D0115692

Mandie and Joe's
Christmas Surprise

Mandie® Mysteries

Mandie and Joe's Christmas Surprise

LOIS GLADYS LEPPARD

BETHANY HOUSE PUBLISHERS
MINNEAPOLIS, MINNESOTA 55438

Published by Bethany House Publishers
A Ministry of Bethany Fellowship, Inc.
11400 Hampshire Avenue South
Bloomington, Minnesota 55438
www.bethanyhouse.com

Printed in the United States of America by
Bethany Press International, Bloomington, Minnesota 55438

Library of Congress Cataloging-in-Publication Data

Leppard, Lois Gladys.
   Mandie and Joe's Christmas surprise / Lois Gladys Leppard.
      p.   cm.
   Summary: When she finds herself in charge of the Christmas Eve skit, Mandie, with Joe's help, tries to remind everyone of the holiday's true meaning by secretly gathering all the town's orphans and giving them parts in the play as well as a home in the church basement. Also includes a script of the story with stage directions.

   [1. Christmas—Fiction. 2. Orphans—Fiction. 3. Christian life—Fiction. 4. Christmas—Drama. 5. Orphans—Drama. 6. Christian life—Drama. 7. Plays.] I. Title.
PZ7.L556Macj   1995
[Fic]—dc20   95-45261
ISBN 1-55661-552-3   CIP
                                                                AC

FOR—

Who else but the other two-thirds of the

Larke Sisters.

LOIS GLADYS LEPPARD has been a professional singer/actress/playwright. She and her two sisters, Sibyl and Louise, sang professionally as the Larke Sisters in New York. The group starred in the operetta *Bohemian Girl* and were presented at Carnegie Hall, among other presentations. She studied at the New York School of Music and at the Voice Beautiful Institute in New York under Glenn Morris Starkie, who had been a student of Enrico Caruso.

As a drama student, she was in the group which organized the present Little Theatre in her hometown. She has written several plays and was at one time with Columbia Pictures. She wrote and had published a song at the age of fifteen. The play in this book was written when she was a young teenager.

Contents

Mandie and Joe's Christmas Secret
A Drama in Three Acts

Part One

Mandie Shaw and Joe Woodard held on to the small hands of four children as they pushed open the basement door of the church across the road from Mandie's house in Franklin, North Carolina.

"Let's go inside now," Mandie told the two little girls she was leading as she gave them a gentle push forward into the large classroom. Joe followed with two small boys.

"How many more do you think we can find?" Joe asked as the two boys pulled away from his grasp, threw off their hats and coats, and headed for a pile of toys in the corner.

Mandie let go of the two little girls after she removed their worn bonnets and coats. They hurried to join the boys who were already examining the playthings. "We need a few more," Mandie replied. "I was hoping we could locate at least a dozen."

"It's going to be hard, if not impossible, to find eight more—especially with Christmas so close," Joe said.

"But we've just got to do it," thirteen-year-old Mandie said, looking at the tall, thin boy who was two years older. "I want this Christmas, in this year of 1901, to be remembered as a *real* Christmas with its true meaning, and this is the way we planned to do it."

"We might could try something else," Joe suggested as he flopped onto a nearby bench.

Mandie sat down beside him as she pushed back the hood of her cape. "But this was the only idea we could come up with," she reminded him. She smoothed back loose tendrils of her long blond hair. She rose, took off her cape, and hung it on a peg in the corner. As she walked over to stand in front of the huge heater in the middle of the room, she said, "We need to build up this fire and get the children warm, don't you think?"

"I'll take care of it," Joe said, jumping up to bring an armful of wood from an alcove nearby. He opened the door of the heater and poked at the burning wood to make room for more. Looking up at Mandie, he asked, "How are we going to do everything that is necessary, just the two of us? I think we need someone to help us. Maybe Liza?"

Mandie frowned as she watched him feed the fire. "I'm not sure we can trust Liza," she said. "I know she wouldn't deliberately give away our secret, but she might just forget and say something to somebody." She thought about the young Negro maid who worked and lived at her uncle's house. The two were friends and had participated in a lot of things together since Mandie's

mother, Elizabeth, had married Mandie's Uncle John after Mandie's father died. But Liza did talk a lot sometimes.

"Who else is there?" Joe asked as he closed the heater door and brushed his hands together.

Mandie walked around the large room a moment and then stopped. "Well, there's my mother, and there's Uncle John. But I don't want them to know what we're doing. What we really need is a wagon so we can go farther out into the country."

"A wagon? The only wagon we'd have a chance of getting belongs to your Uncle John. When my father comes back to your house with my mother, I'm sure he'll be driving the buggy," Joe replied, running his long fingers through his unruly brown hair.

"I sure am glad y'all are spending the holidays with us," Mandie said, looking up at the tall boy with a smile. "I couldn't do all this by myself."

"And I don't think you and I together can do this," Joe replied. "Mandie, we need someone else in on this. For instance, how are we going to take care of all these children down here in the church basement? They have to be fed and will need supervision. We can't just go off and leave them in here all alone."

"I know that, Joe," Mandie said, walking about as she glanced at the children happily playing with rag dolls and balls. "One of us can stay here while the other one goes to find more. And I'm sure I can get plenty of food from our kitchen. And we've got that stack of shuck mattresses in the other room for them to sleep on, plus all those quilts I found in our attic. So I don't see any problem with anything."

Joe sighed as he strolled over to a small window in the far wall to look outside. Mandie followed him.

"Look! It's beginning to snow," Mandie said excitedly as she watched snowflakes fall on the shrubbery right outside the window.

"I think we'd better get some food in here for the night," Joe said as he turned to look at the children.

"All right," Mandie agreed. "It's not quite time for Jenny to begin preparing supper at our house, so while there's no one in our kitchen, I'll make a quick trip over there and bring back whatever I can find."

"Thank goodness you don't have a pastor at this church right now or he'd be sure to catch up with us," Joe remarked.

"The new one won't arrive until February," Mandie said as she put on her cloak and pulled up the hood. "I'll be right back."

"Please hurry back," Joe said as she went out the door.

Mandie hurried around to the front of the church and out into the road. The snowflakes had disappeared. She crossed over to the white fence surrounding the yard of her Uncle John's huge house. Opening the gate, she ran up the walkway and was on the way to the backyard when she heard the sound of horse's hooves pausing on the road.

"Someone is coming," she said to herself as she turned back and saw a buggy stop at the gate. Uncle John's caretaker, Jason Bond, was driving the vehicle, and the passenger was her grandmother, Mrs. Taft. Evidently he had brought her from the depot. Mandie had thought her grandmother was not coming until the next day.

"I have an idea!" Mandie said aloud, lifting her long, heavy skirts as she turned and hurried toward the buggy.

"Grandmother, I'm so glad you're here," Mandie said as Mr. Bond assisted the lady down. Mandie reached to embrace Mrs. Taft.

"I was afraid if I waited any longer we might have a bad snow and I wouldn't be able to get here for Christmas, dear," Mrs. Taft said, returning the hug and straightening her skirts.

Mandie smiled and said, "I don't believe snow would stop you, Grandmother, because the trains do run no matter what the weather is, and Asheville is not so far off anyway."

Mrs. Taft started to walk on toward the front door of the house when Mandie put a hand on her arm to stop her. The old lady looked at her and asked, "What is it, dear?"

Mandie smiled and waited until Mr. Bond had passed them and was well up the walkway before she replied, "Grandmother, I need some help." She paused, not knowing exactly how to explain.

"Help, dear? What kind of help?" Mrs. Taft asked as they stood there on the walkway.

"Well, all kinds of help," Mandie said quickly. "But please understand, Grandmother, what I'm about to tell you is a secret, and you won't give away my secret, will you?"

"Amanda, what on earth are you talking about? It's cold out here and I need to get inside where there's some heat. Now, what is it you want, dear?" Mrs. Taft asked, frowning as she looked at Mandie.

"I'm sorry. I'll hurry up and explain," Mandie said quickly. "You see, Joe Woodard and I have determined that we will make this Christmas a *real* Christmas, the way Jesus' birth ought to be celebrated. And we've made these secret plans, but we need some help. We don't want anyone to know what we're doing, so it will be a big surprise."

"Amanda, what are you and Joe up to? Please hurry and explain," Mrs. Taft said, pulling her cloak closer around her.

"Joe and I asked if we could put on a Christmas play at the church. But nobody knows we are collecting orphans to participate in the play," Mandie quickly explained. "And there are so many angles and odds and ends to this, and only two of us to get it all done. We need someone in on our secret, and I think you are the best secret-keeper I know of."

"Oh dear!" Mrs. Taft said with a loud sigh. "And where are you and Joe getting these orphans?"

"We just brought two little girls from the Swafford farm and two boys from the Pinsons down on Bryson City Road," Mandie explained. "And we are looking for more. We need about twelve to sing and act in the play. But now that we've begun all this, we can see that we need someone to help. Will you, Grandmother? Will you, please?" Mandie's blue eyes looked up at her grandmother.

"Do you mean to say these people just let you take the children off like that?" Mrs. Taft asked.

"Well, they're orphans, Grandmother, and it seems nobody cares about orphans—where they go, what they do. That's why we decided to have no one but orphans in our play. We want everybody to change their attitude toward these little children without mothers and fathers," Mandie explained as she thought about the sad lives of these little ones.

"Amanda, I know you're always trying to do good, but sometimes you have some strange ideas about how to accomplish things," Mrs. Taft said with another big sigh. "What is it you want me to do, dear?"

"Oh, thank you, Grandmother, for understanding," Mandie said, smiling. "Here's what we need. First of all, we need some money to buy wood for the heaters in the church basement, and food for the children, and some of them just have to have warmer clothes. And we need a wagon so we can go on out into the country and find more orphaned children—"

"All right, all right," Mrs. Taft interrupted her. She

shivered and started to walk on toward the house. "Let's get inside before I freeze to death, and we'll discuss this further in my room."

Mandie wondered how she could get food from the kitchen for the children if she spent time with her grandmother. Jenny would soon be preparing the evening meal, and she didn't want Jenny or anyone else to know what she was doing. She quickly decided she would have to go now to get the food.

"Grandmother, I will catch up with you in just a little bit. I had started to the backyard for something. I'll be up to your room by the time you get comfortable." Mandie talked fast, not giving her grandmother a chance to answer as she left the walkway and hurried toward the back of the house.

"All right, Amanda, but don't be too long," Mrs. Taft told her as she walked on toward the front door.

Mandie hurried quietly through the back door and on into the kitchen. There was no one around. She knew where Jenny kept the clean empty flour sacks and she quickly took one from the pantry shelf. Opening the pie safe, she found cornbread, biscuits, and various sweet cakes. On the top shelf was a large bowl of apples.

Grabbing some of each, she dropped them into the flour sack and then raided the icebox, where she found a jug of milk and added it to her bag.

"The warmer," she said softly to herself as she remembered that Jenny sometimes left cooked food in the warmer on the big cast-iron cooking stove. She opened the door and found a pan of fried chicken, still warm and smelling so good. When she pulled out the pan she also found two large baked sweet potatoes.

17

Finally, with the flour sack full, Mandie quickly left by the back door and hurried across the road to the church. As she opened the door, she held out the bag to Joe, who was standing nearby. "Here's the food. I've got to go back for a few minutes. Would you please feed the children? I'll be right back." Before he could protest, she quickly slipped back outside and ran to the house.

She hurried through the front door and down the long hallway to the staircase. Taking the steps two at a time, she rushed upstairs to the room that her grandmother always occupied when she visited them.

She was afraid Mrs. Taft might still be downstairs, so Mandie sighed with relief when her grandmother answered her knock on the door.

"Come in," her grandmother called from inside the room.

Mandie entered and found her grandmother sitting in a comfortable chair with her feet up on a stool by the crackling fire in the fireplace.

"Come on in, dear," Mrs. Taft said, waving her to another stool nearby.

Mandie quickly sat down as she said, "You didn't stay downstairs to visit with my mother."

"No, dear. You said you'd be right back, so I told Elizabeth I needed to rest awhile and would be down for supper," Mrs. Taft said. "Now tell me more about this wild scheme you have concocted."

"Grandmother, I don't think it's exactly a wild scheme," Mandie replied, smiling up at the lady. "Joe and I are hoping the people here in Franklin will join with us in helping the orphans."

"It might work and it might not. Who knows?" Mrs. Taft replied as she watched her granddaughter closely. "Now what is it you want me to do?"

"Like I said before, we need some money and we also need some help in taking care of the orphans until we can present the play," Mandie explained.

"Tell me, how do you think this play will help the orphan situation?" Mrs. Taft asked.

"After the play is over, we are going to ask the audience to make a contribution toward the support of the orphans," Mandie replied. Then she asked quickly, "Grandmother, did you know that people give these orphans a home in order to get free labor? These tiny children who don't have a place to live are farmed out to anyone who is willing to give them a home in exchange for work. Imagine, these small children have to work for their living."

"It is a sorry situation right now, Amanda. I agree on that," Mrs. Taft replied. "But what can you do about it, you and Joe?"

"In the first place, Grandmother, I have experience in being an orphan," Mandie said with a sad look on her face. "Remember how I was sent to the Brysons after my father died because I didn't even know about my real mother? And Uncle Ned came to my rescue. If it hadn't been for him, I suppose I'd still be there working without pay, tending their baby, and not even allowed to go to church. It was horrible, Grandmother." She suddenly remembered that her grandmother had kept her and her mother apart, but Mandie had forgiven her grandmother long ago.

Mrs. Taft stared into the fire and said, "Since it was your father's old Cherokee friend, Uncle Ned, who helped you, have you spoken to him about what you are doing?"

"I haven't seen Uncle Ned since Joe and I decided to do this," Mandie explained. "We've had to act so fast. Christmas is just around the corner, you know."

"Amanda, I would make a couple of suggestions," Mrs. Taft said. "Of course I'll be glad to give you whatever money you need and—"

"Oh, thank you, Grandmother," Mandie interrupted.

"And I think you should ask Liza to help out with this. She would be really good at taking care of the children," Mrs. Taft said.

"Do you think so?" Mandie asked, and when her grandmother nodded she added, "I'm not sure she can keep a secret. Maybe you could explain to her that no one else is to know what we're doing. She would listen to you.''

''I'll see what I can do, but right now I think we'd better go downstairs for supper,'' Mrs. Taft said as she rose.

Mandie jumped up and exclaimed, ''Supper! Oh, Grandmother, what will I do? Joe and I can't both eat supper downstairs at the same time.''

''Then now is the time to find Liza and send her over to the church,'' Mrs. Taft said. ''I'll wait here while you go get her, but make it snappy. Your mother will be wondering where we all are.''

''Yes, Grandmother,'' Mandie said, rushing out the door.

Mandie didn't have far to go. She found Liza folding linens in front of an upstairs hallway closet.

''Quick, Liza, my grandmother wants to talk to you,'' Mandie said, reaching for the young girl's hand.

''Yo' grandmama?'' Liza asked as she allowed herself to be propelled down the corridor to the door of Mrs. Taft's room.

''She'll explain,'' Mandie said, pushing open the door and motioning for Liza to enter the room.

''Lawsy mercy, Missy 'Manda, whut's I done went and done now?'' Liza whispered loudly to Mandie.

Mrs. Taft was waiting just inside the doorway and told Liza, ''We need your help, Liza. Amanda has some children staying in the basement of the church, and we would like for you to watch them while Amanda and Joe eat supper, since you won't be having your meal until later.''

''Chillun in de church?'' Liza questioned as she fidgeted and looked from Mrs. Taft to Mandie.

Mandie knew Liza stood in awe of her grandmother. "That's all you have to do for now," Mandie assured her. "I'll go with you over there."

"But Aunt Lou—whut she gwine say if I run off like dat?" Liza asked.

"Never mind about Aunt Lou," Mrs. Taft said. "I'll fix that. You just run along now with Amanda, and as soon as we have supper she will come and get you."

Mandie knew that Liza considered Mrs. Taft the top authority in anything she was involved in. She watched as Liza shrugged her shoulders and turned to leave the room. "Let's us hurry and git dis ovuh wid," the girl said.

❄ ❄ ❄

Joe was pleased to see Liza when Mandie opened the door to the basement at the church.

"Liza, we sure need your help," he said to the girl.

Liza ignored him and walked over to look at the four children playing in the corner. "Where you git dese heah chillun? Who dey be?" she asked Mandie.

"They're orphans," Mandie said—and then she remembered that Liza didn't have any parents either—"Just like you. They don't have mothers or fathers. We'll explain everything after a while. Right now, please be sure they don't get too close to the heater and they don't go outside. Joe and I will be back just as soon as we can get away from the supper table."

"Dem po' lil' chillun, no mamas and no papas," Liza said. She bent to push back the long dark hair of one little girl. She looked at Mandie and Joe and said, "Y'all jes' git outa heah. We be jes' fine."

Mandie and Joe looked at each other and smiled. "We'll be back real soon," Mandie assured her as she and Joe went out the door.

"I just hope no one goes into the church while we're gone," Mandie said as she and Joe hurried back toward the house.

"There's no reason for anyone to," Joe said.

"You're right. There's nothing scheduled until Sunday, December twenty-second, when we give the play," Mandie agreed.

❄ ❄ ❄

Supper went smoothly. No one seemed to miss Liza, who usually helped wait on the table. Aunt Lou, Uncle John's housekeeper who always supervised, assisted Jenny, the cook, in serving the meal.

As they began eating, Uncle John remarked to Joe, "I suppose your father and mother will be here tomorrow."

"Yes, sir, they should be," Joe replied as he hastily ate.

"And, Amanda, I had a message that Uncle Ned would be visiting us the weekend before Christmas," Uncle John told Mandie.

"Oh, I'm glad, because then he'll be here to see our play that Sunday," Mandie said excitedly, as she thought about what assistance they might need from the old Cherokee.

Elizabeth, Mandie's beautiful young mother, asked,

24

"And this play, Amanda. Have you and Joe decided what you're going to do?"

Mandie and Joe quickly looked at each other. Mandie replied, "Oh, you know, it will be just a regular Christmas play, the usual Christmas story." She cut her eyes at Joe as she hurriedly ate the peas on her plate.

"And will you be needing very many participants?" Uncle John asked, and then added, "In fact, have you two got everything prepared?"

Mrs. Taft looked at Mandie and spoke hurriedly, "From what Amanda tells me, they have it all planned out and it should be enjoyable."

"Fine," Uncle John said. "Then y'all don't need my help."

"Oh, no, thank you, Uncle John, we can manage . . . and you'll be busy with Joe's parents and everything," Mandie said with a big smile.

Uncle John frowned and said, "There is one thing. I have asked Jason Bond to go with the two of you when you get ready to bring in a Christmas tree."

"Thanks, Uncle John. We'll let him know what day we need to get it," Mandie said.

"We'll have to cut two trees, you know," Joe said to Mandie. "One for the play and one for your house here."

"And some holly and mistletoe," Mrs. Taft added with a big smile.

"I just hope we don't get a heavy snowstorm before we get everything in," Mandie said, glancing at Joe. He nodded agreement.

"Why, Amanda, you always wish for a white Christmas," Elizabeth said.

"I know, but if it will just wait until we get everything together for the play and the house decorated," Mandie said, drinking the last of her coffee.

"And our play will be on Sunday, and Christmas isn't until the following Wednesday," Joe added as he ate hurriedly.

"But, remember, we are supposed to go Christmas caroling on Christmas Eve night," Elizabeth reminded them.

"I think you'd better count me out this year," Mrs. Taft said. "I'll stay here and take care of any carolers who come while you're all gone."

Mandie quickly looked at her grandmother. Mrs. Taft had always insisted on participating in everything they did at Christmas time, so she wondered if the lady was up to something.

"Are you not feeling well, Mother?" Elizabeth asked.

"Oh, I'm fine. I just have lots to do. I still haven't purchased all the gifts for everyone, and then I'll have a chance to wrap them without anyone peeking," Mrs. Taft said with a little laugh.

Mandie didn't believe that was the reason. She would just have to keep an eye on her grandmother to find out why she was refusing to go caroling with them.

Supper was finally over, and when Mandie stood up from the table she asked Aunt Lou, who was busy with the coffeepot on the sideboard, "Have you seen Snowball, Aunt Lou?"

"Dat white cat, he done be eatin' his supper in de kitchen whilst y'all been eatin' in heah, my chile," the huge old Negro woman said with a big smile.

"Thanks, Aunt Lou, I'll go see about him," she said, and looking back at Joe she whispered, "I'll take him over for the children to play with."

"Yes, and Liza has to come home and eat," Joe reminded her.

"Mother, Joe and I are going over to do some things at the church," Mandie said to Elizabeth.

"But, dear, your grandmother just got here. Aren't you going to visit with her a while in the parlor with all of us?" Elizabeth asked.

"No, no," Mrs. Taft quickly told her daughter. "We've got plenty of time to visit. After all, I'm going to be here at least two weeks." The old lady looked back at Mandie and winked.

"We won't be gone long, Mother," Mandie promised. "And I'll see you later, Grandmother."

"Well, all right then, but don't be too late," Elizabeth said.

Mandie and Joe hurried to the church and, when they opened the door to the basement, they found Liza and the four children sound asleep. Liza had pushed the benches up against one wall and placed mattresses on them. The two little girls were curled up under a quilt on one mattress and the two boys on the other. Liza herself had gone to sleep in the large chair that was used by a teacher for Sunday school. The lamp in the corner was lit and the heater was crackling away.

"Well!" Mandie whispered as she looked around the room. She smiled at Joe and said, "Liza has done a good job. Let's don't wake them."

"Yes, but she has to go have her supper," Joe reminded her.

Mandie softly walked over to the sleeping girl. She put her hand on her arm and shook her gently. "Liza!" Mandie whispered.

Liza quickly jerked away as she woke up and looked around. She jumped up and said, "Lawsy mercy, Missy 'Manda, I done been asleepin'." She rubbed her eyes and stretched.

"Liza, you need to go back to the house and eat your supper," Mandie said. "When you finish, come on back over here. We want you to spend the night with the children."

"Me spend de night in dis heah spooky church?" Liza asked, her eyes widening as she looked at Mandie.

"Liza, this church is not spooky. It's God's house," Mandie reminded her.

"But I cain't see God. How does I knows He be heah? S'pose de Devil he be heah, too?" Liza said.

"Oh, Liza, the Devil wouldn't dare come into God's house," Mandie said. She looked up at Joe and wondered what they would do if Liza refused to stay at night with the children. "Remember, these little children need you. They don't have any mothers or fathers."

Liza sighed deeply and looked at the sleeping children. "But, Missy 'Manda, I'se jes' plain skeered to stay in dis heah place all night less'n y'all stays too." She moved nervously around the room. "And all dem dead people out dere in de graveyard . . ."

"I'll tell you what, Liza," Joe said. "As soon as everyone in the house goes to bed, I'll come over and sleep in the next room if you'll stay in here with the children."

Liza looked at him and reluctantly replied, "Well, I

s'pose me and dese heah chillun be all right if you sleeps in de next room—but mind you now, if I wakes up and you done gwine left dis heah place, den I be leavin', too."

"Liza, I'll come and stay anytime Joe is not here," Mandie promised. "We won't leave you alone. Now hurry and get your supper before Jenny puts all the food away, and then come right back."

"Well, I guess I be back," Liza said, quickly putting on her hat and coat. She gave them a doubtful look as she went out the door.

Mandie sighed and looked at Joe as soon as the girl had left. "I didn't think about Liza being afraid at night here in the church."

"She'll be all right if she knows one of us is here," Joe said.

"If you want to, we can take turns staying here at night. I could stay tonight, you tomorrow night, and then me, and on like that as long as we have the orphans here," Mandie said as she walked across the long room to keep from waking the children.

"Why don't I stay tonight? You need to talk to your grandmother about a few things, I'm sure," Joe offered. "And then tomorrow night my parents will be here." He followed her to the window where she was standing.

"Yes, I haven't had a chance to let you know that I told Grandmother what we're doing, and she promised to help—I don't know how, but she promised," Mandie explained.

"Why don't you go on back to the house now? There's nothing else to be done tonight, and I'll get one of those mattresses and a quilt and fix me up a place to sleep in the next room," Joe said.

"All right then," Mandie agreed. "But if you need me, let me know. In other words, if Liza has trouble with the children I'll come back and see what I can do."

"Good-night, see you for breakfast," Joe said.

"Bright and early," Mandie replied as she slipped out the door.

Later that night Mandie had a talk with her grandmother in Mrs. Taft's room.

"Sit down, dear," Mrs. Taft told her. She was sitting in the chair by the fireplace again.

Mandie pulled up a stool and waited for her grandmother to begin the conversation.

"You may not like this, but I had to take Aunt Lou into our confidence in order to clear things for Liza," Mrs. Taft began.

Mandie gasped and said, "You told Aunt Lou! Oh, Grandmother, you promised not to let anyone know our secret!"

"There was no other way we could get Liza to help," Mrs. Taft replied. "You know very well that Aunt Lou supervises Liza's duties and has to know where the girl is. But anyhow, Aunt Lou can keep a secret and she thinks you are doing something worthwhile."

"I'm sorry, Grandmother, but I didn't think about Liza's work here in the house," Mandie said, smiling up at the old lady. "And I think our secret is safe with Aunt Lou."

"Now your mother and your Uncle John will be busy shopping and making visits to their friends in preparation for Christmas, so I asked for the use of that rig they keep in the barn and never use. That way they can use the buggy and we'll have the rig anytime we want it. I couldn't figure out how to ask for use of the wagon, but the rig is better anyway."

"So I suppose Abraham will harness it up for us when we get ready to use it," Mandie said. "Joe and I want to go out into the country tomorrow and try to find more orphans."

"That's fine," Mrs. Taft said. "Liza can watch the children and I will check on her now and then, and Aunt Lou has offered to help in any way we need her. Your mother and your Uncle John will be gone to the Lawsons all day. And I'll be here when Dr. Woodard and his wife arrive."

"Grandmother, Liza was afraid to stay all night in the church, so Joe has to sleep over there tonight and I will tomorrow night, and we'll take turns until we have the play," Mandie said.

"You and Joe are going to have a job returning all those orphans to their homes if you bring in too many," her grandmother warned her.

"Well, we thought since the play is on a Sunday and Christmas is not until the following Wednesday, we would just keep the children in the church until after Christmas," Mandie told her.

"Don't you think that's a little too much, having those children that long and having to take care of them?" Mrs. Taft asked.

Mandie smiled up at her grandmother and said, "Well, I was hoping we could buy them some presents and have a real Christmas for them on Christmas Day, with lots of toys and lots of food and some warm clothes. That is part of what we need money for."

31

"Amanda, you're always planning something," Mrs. Taft said, and then she smiled at Mandie. "I'll go shopping with you and I'll even volunteer to wrap the presents if you wish."

Mandie reached to squeeze her grandmother's hand as she said, "I knew I could depend on you."

"I don't know what you all are planning to do for costumes for the children, but I would suggest asking Aunt Lou to help with that. You know she's a wonderful seamstress," Mrs. Taft said.

"Yes, she is," Mandie replied. "I'm so glad you are helping us. And it was a good idea to let Aunt Lou in on our secret."

Mrs. Taft stood up and said, "You run along to bed now. I need to get some sleep, too. Just let me know when you need me for anything."

"Good-night, Grandmother, and thanks," Mandie said as she tiptoed to kiss the old lady's cheek.

Mrs. Taft quickly embraced her, and Mandie went to her own room.

Part Two

Early the next morning Mandie hurriedly dressed and rushed over to the church to check on the situation. Liza and the children were all awake, but Joe was nowhere in sight when Mandie looked into the room where he had put his mattress.

"Where is Joe?" Mandie asked.

"He say he gwine to de house to git food," Liza replied as she watched the orphans play with the toys.

"Oh goodness, I have to go see what he's doing. I'll be right back," Mandie said as she rushed back out the door.

She went to the back door of the house because she figured Joe would be in the kitchen if he was looking for food. When she pushed open the door, she found Aunt Lou and Jenny cooking and Joe standing by watching.

"Joe!" Mandie said as she looked around the room,

not sure what to make of the scene. Had someone let Jenny in on their secret, too?

"Mawnin, my chile," Aunt Lou greeted her as she turned and smiled at Mandie.

"Good morning, Aunt Lou and Jenny," Mandie said. "And Joe."

"Mawnin' Missy 'Manda," Jenny said as she turned bacon cooking in the big iron frying pan. "We'se almost done wid dem chillun's breakfast."

Joe looked at Mandie and said, "It was too complicated trying to feed the orphans, so I took the liberty of letting Jenny in on our secret, and your grandmother had already told Aunt Lou."

"Well," Mandie replied, not knowing exactly what to say. Pretty soon it wouldn't be a secret at all. Everyone would know what they were doing, she was thinking.

"Now don't you worry, my chile, we'se ain't tellin' nobody else," Aunt Lou said as she bent to pull a pan of hot biscuits out of the oven.

"No, we won't," Jenny quickly added. "But we all wants to he'p anyhow. It be a good thing y'all doin'." She began removing the crisp bacon and laying it out on a plate.

"And I appreciate y'all's help," Mandie said, finally smiling. Turning to Joe, she said, "Liza and the children are all up, and I came looking for you so we could get breakfast for them."

"We don't have any more problems about food," Joe said. "Aunt Lou and Jenny will see to every meal for us."

"Thank you, both," Mandie told the women. "Is there anything I can do to help?"

"No, my chile. You and Mistuh Joe heah jes' git ready fo' yo' own breakfus' 'cause Abraham gwine run dis food over to de chilluns," Aunt Lou told her.

Mandie looked at Joe and said, "So Abraham knows, too?"

"We couldn't figure out how to cook two meals and serve them, so it was Jenny's idea to get her husband to carry the food over to the church every time we eat," Joe explained.

Mandie sighed deeply and said, "We're getting obligated to so many people."

"No sech thing, my chile," Aunt Lou protested as she buttered the biscuits. "We wants to he'p dese chilluns, jes' like you be doin'. Now like I done said, you two git washed up and ready fo' yo' own breakfus'."

She flapped her long white apron at Mandie and Joe. "Shoo!"

Both the young people laughed and Mandie said, "All right, thank you."

"Thanks," Joe added.

He followed Mandie out the door into the hallway. As they hurried down the long corridor Mandie said, "Any problems last night?"

"None at all. As far as I know, Liza and the children slept straight through, but let me tell you, they were all up early this morning. I more or less dozed all night on that uncomfortable mattress, and as soon as I dropped off to sleep, Liza woke me with her yelling, laughing, and playing with the children," Joe explained. "She is really enjoying this."

"I'm glad," Mandie said as they reached the staircase. "Let's sit down here a minute and I'll tell you what all my grandmother has planned."

They sat on the bottom step and Mandie brought him up to date.

"So how are we going to get the rig out without your mother and Uncle John knowing about it, when your grandmother asked permission to use it for herself?" Joe asked.

"We'll just wait until my mother and Uncle John leave for the Lawsons, and then we'll take the rig and go looking for more orphans," Mandie explained.

So that is what they did. Mandie's mother and Uncle John left as soon as everyone ate breakfast. Abraham harnessed one of the horses to the rig, then Mandie and Joe began their search for more orphans. By noontime they had found six more children, four girls and two boys. The boys were brothers but did not know each other because they had been placed with different families when they were babies.

Mrs. Oglesby had said, "This boy here, Jake, has a brother living with the Houstons across the river there. But they don't know each other. We tried to take both boys when their parents died, but the Houstons insisted they found Jasper first and wouldn't give him up. We offered them the chance to take Jake because we didn't like to separate brothers, but they only wanted one child. That was when the boys were babies. Jake is six now and Jasper is five."

Mandie stood there in Mrs. Oglesby's yard listening with a heavy heart to the story of the separated brothers. "Do you suppose the Houstons would allow Jasper to come with us for the Christmas holidays?" she asked.

"They might," Mrs. Oglesby told her. "Provided you don't let them know you have Jasper's brother, too."

Joe looked back at the rig where the children were waiting and said, "That would really be a wonderful Christmas present to the boys to find each other."

Mrs. Oglesby's thin face lit up and she said, "It would be. Bless you young people. I'll be praying for you."

Mandie said a silent prayer herself as Joe pulled the rig up in the yard of the Houstons' home. A young boy, almost identical in looks to Jake, was swinging on a rope swing hanging from a huge chestnut tree. Mandie knew at once that he was Jasper.

"Jasper, is anyone home besides you?" Mandie called to him as she and Joe stepped down from the rig.

"Them people Houstons, what I live with here, they be home." Jasper jumped down from the swing and approached the rig.

"Where are they?" Joe asked. "We'd like to talk to them."

"They down at the river at the still. They always tell me I ain't supposed to go down there, but I know what they're doin'. They're makin' that strong stuff what makes people wobble," Jasper explained.

Mandie and Joe looked at each other.

"If he can't go down there and get them and we don't know where the still is, how are we going to talk to them?" Mandie asked as Jasper walked around her and stood staring at the children in the rig. She noticed they stared back.

"Maybe he could explain where it is and I could find it," Joe suggested. Turning to Jasper he asked, "Could you show me the way to the still? You don't have to go down there. Just tell me how to find it."

Jasper stood kicking the dirt and looking down at his feet for a moment. Then he straightened up and said, "Shucks, everyone knows where it be. But I'll show you. Come this way." He hurried down an overgrown pathway by the side of the barn and stopped to see if Joe was following.

"I'm coming," Joe told him as he caught up with Jasper. He called back to Mandie, "Don't let those children out of your sight. We're responsible for them, remember."

"I won't," Mandie promised.

Mandie waited a long time in the yard. She walked around and around, watching every move the children in the rig made. Finally she spotted Joe coming back up the lane. Jasper was skipping along ahead of him, and an elderly woman walked behind Joe on the narrow path.

Jasper ran ahead and went back to stand and stare at the children in the rig. The woman kept talking as she came closer, and Mandie could finally hear what she was saying.

"The boy ain't worth his salt, but we keep him anyhow," she was saying. "We ain't got no children of our own."

Then Mandie heard Joe ask, "Did y'all adopt the boy?"

The woman stopped and put her hands on her hefty hips as she said, "My goodness, no. We don't call him as part of the family. He just gets to live here in exchange for a few chores he does, and that ain't much."

Mandie walked over to meet Joe and the woman when they reached the yard.

"This is Amanda Shaw, Mrs. Houston," Joe said.

Mandie smiled and said, "How do you do, Mrs. Houston?"

The woman stared at Mandie from head to toe and said, "Right poorly, if I do have to say so. Y'all jes' wait here and I'll git him a change of clothes, which is about all he's got. I'll be right back."

The woman went on into the house, and Mandie and Joe stood by the rig while Jasper continued to stare at the other children.

"Was it really what he said it was?" Mandie asked in a low voice to prevent Jasper from hearing her.

"Sure was. It's a wonder we don't smell it all the way

up here," Joe said. "The woman's husband and his brother take care of it. They didn't seem upset when I walked up and asked for the Houstons. They just wanted to know what I was after, and when they were sure I wasn't a lawman, they agreed Jasper could go home with us for Christmas, even though we are strangers. The woman said it would give her a rest from continually scolding Jasper and trying to make him work."

Mandie whispered, "They are terrible people, aren't they? I wonder if they beat the boy."

"It's possible from the way they talked," Joe said.

The woman came out of the house with a stuffed flour sack and handed it to Joe. "This ought to be enough to last till he gits back," she said. "Now, I got to git back to work. Jes' bring him on back when y'all git ready." She hurried back down the pathway.

Mandie turned to look at Jasper, and she saw that he had been listening. "Come on, Jasper, we're going to visit some other people," she told him as she reached to take his hand. He quickly pulled his hand away and drew back from her. "Jasper, don't you want to ride in this rig and talk to these other children?"

The boy stood still and looked from Mandie to the rig and then at Joe. He suddenly ran to Joe's side. "I'll ride with him," he said, frowning at Mandie.

"All right," Joe said. "You can sit on the front seat with me and Mandie." He lifted the boy and set him down inside. Mandie got in from the other side.

When they were all seated and Joe had picked up the reins, Jasper edged closer to Joe and gave Mandie a stern look. The other children were silently watching and listening. Very little was said until Joe drove the rig

40

into town. Then the children all became excited and started talking. Evidently none of them had ever been in town before.

"Are we going to church?" Jake asked loudly as Joe pulled the rig around behind the church.

Mandie smiled and said softly to Joe, "At least one of them knows what a church is."

"No, we're not exactly going to church," Joe explained as he tied the reins. "You see, we're going to live in the church for a while."

The children jumped down to the ground and one of the girls asked, "Live in a church? Nobody but *God* lives in a church."

Mandie stooped to quickly embrace the little dark-haired, dark-eyed six-year-old girl and said, "Well, He's going to let us live in here for a little while. Come on. There are more children already here."

As Mandie opened the door to the church, the children inside stopped their playing to stare at the children outside. No one moved, and Mandie had to give each one a little push to get them all to enter.

Liza watched and then suddenly asked, "Well, I hope I never! Them be twins you got dere?"

Mandie looked at her and saw she was watching Jake and Jasper. Now that they were standing together she could see a strong resemblance between the two. "No," Mandie told Liza as she looked back at Joe, who had come in behind her. He shook his head, and she understood they wouldn't give away the fact that Jake and Jasper were brothers.

"Now we has to git dese coats and thangs off," Liza

told the new children as she began removing their wraps.

Mandie and Joe helped until Jake said loudly, "A ball!" He ran to pick it up from the middle of the other toys. That finally broke the silence and the other children hastily threw off their coats and hats and raced to join him. Then it became noisy.

"Whew!" Mandie said, blowing out her breath.

"Amen!" Joe said with a little laugh.

Liza added, "Y'all can say dat agin."

The three watched as the children played with the toys and talked to each other.

"We'd better see about their dinner," Mandie said.

"Dey done et," Liza told her. "Jenny done been over and fed 'em. Said she wanted to let dem eat first."

"Then we'd better go find us something to eat," Mandie said. "Liza, have you eaten?"

"I sho' has, Missy 'Manda," Liza said, smiling. "I et wid de chilluns."

"Then we'll go and come right back so you can take some time off away from the children. You're probably tired of them by now," Mandie said.

"Lawsy mercy, Missy 'Manda, I don't be tired of dese heah chilluns. I'se been havin' a good time playin' wid dem and if I goes back to de house, Aunt Lou she put me to work. I druther stay right heah," Liza said as she danced around the room.

Mandie laughed and said, "All right, Liza, but we will be back in a little while to make some plans for the play."

"I wonder if the children we brought with us have had their dinner," Joe said.

Mandie and Joe questioned the new children, and they all claimed to have already had their noon meal.

"That's strange, because it's just now a little after twelve, and we picked up the girls a lot earlier," Mandie said.

"Why don't we just bring them back some cake and milk or something?" Joe asked. "That way we'll at least know they won't be hungry till suppertime."

"Good idea," Mandie said. Looking back at Liza, she teased, "Too bad you already ate."

"But we had chocolate cake, too." Liza said, grinning at her.

"Sounds like we'd better hurry and see if Aunt Lou has given away all our chocolate cake," Mandie said as she rushed out the door ahead of Joe.

When they reached the house they found that Dr. and Mrs. Woodard had already arrived and were just sitting down to eat with Mrs. Taft.

"Sorry, we're almost late," Mandie said as she rushed into the dining room after leaving her cloak on the hall tree. Joe was right behind her.

The two sat down across from the Woodards. Mrs. Taft was sitting at the head of the table, since Mandie's mother and Uncle John were not expected back until late in the day.

"Did y'all get all your errands done?" Mrs. Taft asked, looking directly at Mandie and then at Joe.

"I think we've finished. We gave Abraham the rig." Mandie said, glancing at Joe.

"That's good. Now Mrs. Woodard and I will do some shopping this afternoon," Mrs. Taft said as Aunt Lou and Jenny began serving the food.

44

"And I have a patient I need to see," Dr. Woodard added.

"That's fine," Joe told them. "We can all sit down and visit tonight."

Mandie needed to get together with Aunt Lou to begin making the children's costumes for the play. So she was glad everyone was going to be out.

The minute everyone had finished the meal, Mandie rushed back into the kitchen to tell Jenny she wasn't sure the children they had brought in that morning had had any food since breakfast.

"Jes' you leave it to me," Jenny told her. "I'll fix up a big basket and take it over myself. I needs to check on Liza anyhow, and I'll do this right now 'fo I cleans up de table."

"Thanks, Jenny," Mandie said. "I'll rid up the table with Aunt Lou while you're gone. I need to talk to her."

The adults left immediately after the meal, so Joe volunteered to help. Aunt Lou fussed and tried to refuse the young people's help, but they insisted.

"I knows how to clean up food and dirty dishes," Aunt Lou grumbled as she began scraping and stacking the plates. "I don't need no 'sistance."

"I know, Aunt Lou, but this will give us a chance to talk," Mandie told her as she began collecting the water glasses. "Besides, you and Jenny have to eat, too, you know, and the faster we get all this into the kitchen, the sooner y'all can eat."

The three of them had everything in the kitchen in a few minutes. Then Mandie looked up at Aunt Lou and said, "My grandmother told me you were willing to help us with the children and the play."

"Dat's right, my chile," Aunt Lou said, wiping her hands on her big white apron. "Now what is it I can do?"

"We need some costumes for the children," Mandie began.

"And we have six girls and four boys," Joe added.

"And I think that is all the children we're going to find," Mandie said, looking at Joe, who nodded.

"So I s'pose you be needin' some lil angel clothes, or sumpin' like dat," Aunt Lou said.

"Yes, I think we might as well dress them all as angels because they're going to sing together," Mandie said.

"Liza been teachin' 'em to sing?" the old woman asked.

Mandie looked at her in surprise. Of course, Liza would be the perfect teacher. She had a beautiful voice and she knew every song anyone could mention.

"Thanks for saying that, Aunt Lou. I was wondering how we would teach the children any songs, but of course they love Liza already, and I'm sure she could do the best job," Mandie said.

"And I'll make the white costumes," said Aunt Lou. "I'll jes' have to go over and measure 'em all up."

"Oh, thank you, Aunt Lou," Mandie said as she quickly embraced the big woman. "What a load off us. Then Joe and I will write the play and decorate the church, and we'll have to go shopping for Christmas presents for the children."

The next few days went fast. While Mandie's mother, Elizabeth, and her Uncle John entertained Dr. Woodard and Mrs. Woodard, everyone else was secretly working on the Christmas presentation. Jason Bond, the caretaker, helped Mandie and Joe bring in Christmas trees, one for the house and one for the church. Then the whole household pitched in and decorated the tree in the house. Mandie insisted she and Joe didn't need any help on the one in the church because she wanted the orphans to participate in that job, and she was afraid someone else would discover their secret.

"We need to practice," Mandie told Joe one night when they went over to the church to see how Liza was doing at teaching songs.

"Definitely," Joe agreed. "And we need to rehearse everything."

When they opened the door to the church, they found Liza and the orphans lined up across the room practicing their songs. Mandie was amazed at how well they were doing.

Mandie and Joe took everyone into the sanctuary of the church for the first time and explained to the children that they were to help decorate the tree on the stage. They squealed with delight as they fastened decorations to the tree. Liza giggled right along with them.

"Now you will all stand up there on the stage and sing, and people will be sitting down in the audience listening to you," Mandie explained. "Liza, let's try them out and see how they are going to act."

"Dey does fine, Missy 'Manda," Liza replied. She placed them in the center of the stage and they began singing "Silent Night."

Mandie and Joe sat in front and watched and listened. When the children were finished, Mandie said, "They need some music. It would sound so much better. And I don't know where we're going to get someone to play the piano."

"That's something you need to learn to do," Joe told Mandie. "You'd think that fancy school you go to in Asheville would have taught you by now." He grinned at her.

"Oh, Joe, my mother has already said I have to learn, and I'm getting a late start," Mandie agreed. "Now I wish I did know how to play." She sighed.

"Well, I guess I could help you out on that, although I don't want to," Joe said, quickly getting up and walking over to raise the lid of the piano as he sat down on the swivel stool. Before Mandie could say a word he ran down the keyboard and began playing "Silent Night."

Mandie was speechless. She went over to stand by the piano. And Liza had the children sing right along with him.

As soon as he hit the last note, Mandie asked loudly,

"Joe Woodard! When did you learn to play the piano?"

Joe grinned at her and said, "A long, long time ago."

Mandie frowned and said, "I've known you all my life, and I didn't know you could play a piano. Why have you been so secretive about it?"

"I haven't been," Joe said. "My mother taught me as soon as I could walk, just about. But I revolted after I got up in school."

Mandie grinned at him and said, "I'm glad to find this out about you. I'm sure we can make use of your talent for this play."

"Well, I don't know about that," Joe protested. "I'm not very good."

"I know better than that," Mandie said. "If you can play one Christmas song I'm sure you can play the rest we want to sing."

Liza and the children were standing around watching and listening. Joe suddenly stood and closed the lid on the piano. Mandie reached past him and opened it. Turning to Liza she said, "Tell him what else to play for the children."

Liza hurriedly named off several songs and Joe played them while the children sang. Finally Mandie noticed the little orphans were growing sleepy, and she suddenly realized it must be past their bedtime.

"It's time to quit for the night," Mandie said. "Liza, let's take the children back to their room and get them ready for bed."

"And since it's your night to stay here, I'd better be going," Joe said as he followed them into the basement.

"Thanks for playing, Joe," Mandie told him as they entered the room where the children slept. "And you will play for the children during our presentation, won't you?" She smiled up at him.

Joe shuffled his feet and finally replied, "Only if I can wear a costume to disguise myself so no one will know who I am."

"Of course, that's a wonderful idea," Mandie said. "Think up an idea of what you want to wear and I'll get Aunt Lou to make it."

"All right. See everybody in the morning," Joe said as he went out the door and a string of good-nights followed him.

Mandie helped Liza get the children to bed. Then Liza curled up on her own mattress, and Mandie sat down by the lamp at the far end of the long room with her notebook to go over what had been accomplished and what needed to be done. It wasn't really late, only nine o'clock when she looked at her watch, but she soon started dozing off in her chair after everyone got quiet.

Mandie was startled awake by someone opening the outside door. She scrambled to her feet, rubbing her eyes and trying to focus her vision on the person. It was a man, a strange man! She quickly realized if she yelled she'd wake the children and terrify them, and Liza would be wild with fear. So she walked toward him across the length of the long room. He seemed to be standing still.

As she got nearer, she saw he was a tall, handsome man, probably in his forties, with dark curly hair. And as she came close enough to look into his eyes, she dis-

covered they were a deep blue and seemed to be full of surprise.

"I'm sorry," the man said. He looked around the room. "I didn't know someone was using the basement. You see, I've just got back into town after many long years and thought I'd run over to visit my old church where I went as a child."

"Oh!" Mandie said with a gasp. She straightened her skirts and stood up taller. Luckily she had not changed into her nightclothes. "I see. My name is Amanda Shaw, Mandie for short, and these children are all orphans." She waved her hand around the room at the sleeping children.

"I apologize. I'm George Simpson," he informed her. "Are you related to Mr. John Shaw?"

Mandie looked at him in surprise as she replied, "Yes, he is my uncle and he married my mother after my father, Jim Shaw, died."

"Well, well, well!" the man said, with a big smile. "I remember your father very well before he married your mother. After that he seemed to disappear, but Mr. John Shaw was very kind to me when I was growing up. You see, I was an orphan, too."

"If you were an orphan, where did you live here in Franklin when you attended this church?" Mandie anxiously asked.

"Oh, here and there, mostly with my mother's old cousins, who have just died. That's why I'm back in town," George explained.

"Did I know them? Who were they?" Mandie asked.

"No, you probably didn't know them, because they left town years ago to live over in Jackson County," he said. "They owned the huge house on the hill just as you go around the curve on Bryson City Road. It has been closed up ever since they moved away, and I find it's in bad shape. I am their only heir and they left it to me, and I don't know what I'll be doing with it."

"Don't you want to live in it? I know the house you're talking about. It looks like a mansion, it's so big," Mandie said.

"No, it would be impossible for me to live here in Franklin," George said. "You see, I have a home in New York and my business is up there, so I don't need the house."

"New York?" Mandie questioned. "I've never been there, but someday I will go. Couldn't you move your business down here so you could live in the house? I'm sure it would be beautiful if someone would fix it up."

George laughed and said, "No, I couldn't do that. I'm an actor and I have to stay where the theater is."

Mandie did some quick thinking. "These children are here temporarily so we can have them in a Christmas play here in the church. My friend Joe Woodard and I are presenting the play the Sunday before Christmas, next Sunday in fact. Could we persuade you to act in our play? Please." Her blue eyes looked directly into his.

George laughed and said, "Sorry. I won't be in Franklin this coming weekend. I will return next week to do something about the house, though."

Mandie had another idea. "How much are you going to sell the house for? I mean, you must be planning to sell it since you don't want it."

George looked down at her and asked, "Why? Do

you know of someone who might be interested in buying it? I don't believe it's worth much.''

Mandie laughed and said, "No, not exactly. I was just thinking what a perfect home it would make for these orphans here. You see, they've all been farmed out wherever a family needs them to do work, and I'm sure they're being mistreated. Can you imagine little ones like these having to work for their keep?''

George Simpson turned to pace about the end of the room. Then he stopped and looked at Mandie. "Yes, I know exactly what it's like. I went through all that and somehow managed to survive. I ran away from the last place that gave me a home, because they beat me. I was fourteen and I hitchhiked—walked most of the way, really—to New York. I got various backbreaking jobs and was able to get some education. Then when I was seventeen, I got really lucky. I landed a job as a driver for one of the big Broadway producers, and he gave me my start in show business. But I am well aware that not all orphans are given an opportunity like that.''

Mandie thought about herself, how she had been farmed out to work for the Brysons when her father died, but she didn't want to sidetrack the conversation so she didn't mention it.

"I'm sorry, Mr. Simpson, but I'm happy for you now," Mandie said, smiling up at him. "Don't you think the house would be a good place to put these orphans?''

George thought for a moment and said, "Yes, I agree. I remember being in the house. It probably has twenty rooms. But it's in bad shape right now.''

Mandie frowned and walked around. If he would allow the orphans to live there, what could she do about making the house fit to live in? If he would donate the house, where could she get the money to renovate it? From the people of Franklin, of course! She would solicit donations from the members of this church when the children put on the play.

Excitedly she turned back to George. "I know what we could do! If you would give us the house for the orphans, I could probably get the money from the townspeople to fix it up."

"But what about maintenance? How would you run the operation? After all, there are regular bills, such as food and clothing among other things, that have to be funded from somewhere," George replied.

Mandie said a silent prayer and she looked up to face George Simpson. "If you will donate the house to the orphans, I will come up with the money to run it. I have faith in the people's kindness here in Franklin, and above all, I have faith that God will supply it." She clasped her hands as she waited for his answer.

With a big grin on his face George Simpson stepped up and held out his hand. "It's a deal," he said. "You get the money rounded up and I will be back in town, probably on Christmas Eve, and we'll seal the bargain."

Mandie, overcome with excitement and thankfulness, suddenly raised up on tiptoes and planted a kiss on the man's cheek. "Thank you, with all my heart, thank you!" she exclaimed with tears of joy in her eyes.

George embraced her quickly and said, "Now I have to go. I have someone waiting for me. I will see you on Christmas Eve." He started toward the door.

"Thank you," Mandie said again as she followed him to the door.

He went out, and she shut the door and leaned against it, too excited to go to bed now. It was going to be a long night. She would have to wait for daybreak to come so she could rush over and tell Joe.

The Lord was going to take care of His orphans.

Part Three

The next morning, by the time Mandie spread the word to everyone involved in the Christmas play secret, she was almost too hoarse to speak.

Mrs. Taft remembered being in the huge house when people lived there and she told Mandie that, as far as she could recollect, the owners had grown too old to care for George Simpson and had lost everything but their house. Then they had moved over to Jackson County to stay with other relatives when the boy was probably six or seven years old.

"Yes, Amanda, it would be an ideal place for the orphans to live, but just remember it takes money to keep up such a place, as the man said," Mrs. Taft told her, as they sat in her bedroom early that morning.

"But I am going to ask all the people in Franklin to donate money, or if they can't afford that, to donate time for fixing up the house and taking care of the children," Mandie explained.

"Well, I hope you will be able to do that, Amanda, but please don't build up too much hope. It's a doubtful proposition," her grandmother said.

"I just believe I can do it," Mandie said. She jumped up from the footstool where she sat and said, "Now I've got to see if Joe is downstairs yet so I can tell him."

Joe was in the kitchen hungrily watching Aunt Lou and Jenny prepare breakfast. When Mandie came in the door, he and the two women all looked at her.

"You're out so early. Is everything all right over at the church?" Joe asked anxiously.

"Fine. In fact, finer than normal," Mandie said with a big laugh as she twirled around the room. "I have exciting news. I've found a new home for the orphans."

"A home?" Joe inquired.

"Is dat so?" Aunt Lou said.

"Praise de Lawd!" Jenny shouted as she clapped her hands.

"Yes," Mandie said, and she went on to explain about the visit of George Simpson. No one said a thing until she had finished. "So now all we have to do is get money and work from the people of Franklin."

"Good luck," Joe said with a sigh.

"Now that's no attitude to take," Mandie reprimanded him. "We just have to trust and have faith and we can do it. I know we can."

"I give time, my chile, but ain't got no money," Aunt Lou said.

Mandie ran to embrace her as she said, "There! That's our first donation."

"And I'll he'p cook for dem chillun, jes' like we doin' now," Jenny promised.

Mandie hugged her and said, "You see, it's going to work. We can do it."

"I'll do whatever I can, but I don't even live in Franklin, Mandie, and I won't be here to give much time," Joe reminded her.

"We will accept the very smallest donation of time, work, or money," Mandie declared.

❊ ❊ ❊

Saturday night finally came and Mandie and Joe worked late to be sure everything would be ready for the play the next day. Decorations were checked. Costumes were pressed. The children practiced their songs. And Mandie wrote a speech which she planned to deliver to the audience after the play was over.

Sunday morning Mandie woke to find a light snow had fallen the night before, but it would not deter the people from getting to church. It only made it seem more Christmas-like.

At the breakfast table Elizabeth asked, "Shall we go over to the church when you do, dear, and maybe help get things in order for the play?"

"Oh, no, Mother, we don't need you. I mean we have everything in order and we appreciate your offer, but please don't come over until everyone else starts coming in," Mandie said, quickly looking at Joe.

"You seem awfully mysterious about all this," Uncle John commented as he ate his food.

"Yes, and I know these two well enough to know the

outcome of their secrecy is always unpredictable," Dr. Woodard said with a laugh.

"Oh, well, you know how young people are," Mrs. Taft said as she looked around the table. "They just like to do things on their own, without some grownup telling them what to do. I imagine the play will be interesting."

"Yes, I'm sure it will be," Mrs. Woodard remarked.

Mandie just remembered something and she asked, "I thought Uncle Ned was coming to see us this weekend."

"Oh, he is," Uncle John said. "He'll be here in time for your play, at the regular morning worship time."

Mandie had been hoping he would get there before the play. Now she would have to postpone a talk with him until afterward.

The two young people rushed through the meal and asked to be excused in order to get last minute details ready in the church.

When Mandie told the children that this was the big day, that they would be dressed in their costumes and would sing before a real audience, some of them got excited. Jake and Jasper had become good friends and were ready for anything, but she noticed two of the little girls seemed shy.

Mandie and her grandmother had bought gifts for all the children and they were now wrapped and beneath the huge tree on the stage. Excitement ran through Mandie's heart as she anticipated the happiness of the orphans when they unwrapped toys and clothes all their own.

Aunt Lou and Jenny had slipped over to the church to help, and finally it was time.

The church had a large platform, and with the help of Aunt Lou and Abraham, Mandie and Joe had converted it into a real stage. Aunt Lou had made a curtain out of bedsheets and Joe and Abraham had hung them on rods across the front, concealing the stage to the audience until the curtains would be pulled back by ropes at each side.

When the curtain was finally pulled before a full audience—with some standing in the back—Mandie began reading the story of Jesus' birth as she sat on a low stool by the huge Christmas tree. She wore a long red dress and had pinned a bunch of holly with red berries on her shoulder. Her hair was loose, flowing down below her waist.

As she recited the story, the children came onto the stage with Liza, all dressed in white robes with wings and halos, and they began to sing softly in the background.

Then Abraham, dressed as Joseph, and Jenny, dressed as Mary, entered from backstage.

All this time Joe was softly playing the piano, which they had moved into a dark corner by the stage. He was clothed in a robe and his head was covered with a turban.

While she was reading, Mandie's eyes danced around the stage as she tried to ascertain that everything was going as planned. It had taken a lot of persuasion to get Jenny and her husband, Abraham, to participate, and she had to agree that they would not have to learn any lines or speak.

The audience was completely silent until the moment when the curtain closed, and then they applauded

as the church had never heard before. Aunt Lou was pulling the curtain, and she kept opening and closing it for everyone to bow until Mandie signaled her to stop.

Mandie took the orphans downstage and held up her hand to speak. She had them lined up for the audience to see.

"Ladies and gentlemen, I would like to tell you how much we appreciate your coming and how much the applause meant to us for all the hard work involved, but I just wanted to explain a few things," she began as the crowd became quiet and sat back down.

"We wanted to make this a real Christmas—what Christmas really stands for—Jesus' birthday, not just the time when Santa Claus comes and everyone is so anxious to receive all the gifts they can get, with no mention of our Savior. Presents should be given to show our love for other people, people who are poor and needy, and who won't receive much for Christmas."

She paused when she spotted Uncle Ned sitting in the audience. She felt like waving at him, but she only smiled as she continued.

"These little children are all orphans. They don't have homes. They live wherever people will take them in exchange for work. Imagine little ones like these having to work for their keep," she continued. "I want to ask each and every one of you to help these orphans. You probably all know about the old house that's been closed up for years and years out on Bryson City Road. Well, the owners died recently and I met the man who has inherited it, George Simpson, their cousin." She paused as some of the older people looked at each other in recognition of the name.

Mandie took a deep breath and continued as she said a silent prayer. "Now Mr. Simpson has agreed to give us the house for a home for these orphans, provided we donate enough time, work, and money to get it in livable shape and maintain it. Just look at these two little boys here named Jake and Jasper. They are not aware of it yet, but they were separated when they were babies after the death of their parents. That shouldn't ever happen to anyone." She pointed to the boys, who stared at each other and rushed to embrace.

There was a murmur from the audience. Mandie looked at the left edge of the stage and saw Joe hiding behind the curtain as he listened to what she was saying. He gave her a big grin and she turned back to continue.

"Now I'm asking that every person in this audience give something," Mandie said. Her voice got stern as her determination grew. "Everybody here can give something. If you don't have money to give, you can give time and work. We have promised Mr. Simpson that the people of Franklin will come to the rescue of these little orphans, and we are going to keep our promise. Please don't say you're too busy or you can't afford to give even a few dollars. No matter how poor you are, you can still share in some way. We can always find someone poorer than we are, and these little orphans are poorer than anyone in this audience."

She paused again to let that soak in, and then she continued.

"Now who will be the first to make a donation?" she asked, as she looked over the audience. The crowd had become restless and the people were murmuring among themselves.

Suddenly a heavyset man with bushy gray hair stood up and yelled at Mandie, "We don't need a half-breed telling us what to do with our money and time!"

Mandie was so shocked she yelled back, "I am what God made me and I can't change that so you better like it!"

Joe instantly came to her side and shouted to the man, "This is God's house and no place for such talk, mister!"

Uncle Ned suddenly materialized at Mandie's side and, putting his arm around her, managed to get her behind the curtain. Joe followed.

They could hear the audience picking up on what the man said. "No, we don't." "No." "Never." Finally the uproar grew dimmer and Mandie knew the people were leaving the church.

"Papoose!" Uncle Ned said as he tightly embraced Mandie. Aunt Lou, Jenny, Abraham, and Liza all surrounded them with shocked expressions.

In spite of her determination, Mandie felt her eyes flood with tears and she turned to lean her head on the old Cherokee's shoulder. The others were softly murmuring to comfort her. The orphans stood in awe and watched.

In a moment, Mandie's grandmother had come onto the stage. Elizabeth and Uncle John and Dr. and Mrs. Woodard were close behind them. Mandie dimly saw Jason Bond bringing up the rear as they all came toward her.

"I'll fix that man!" Mrs. Taft was so angry, she was sputtering.

"Are you all right, dear?" Elizabeth asked as she patted Mandie's blond head.

Mandie looked up at her mother, and making every effort to steady her voice, she said, "I'm all right, Mother. I just need to get everything straightened up here so we can go eat dinner."

"Please hurry, dear," Elizabeth told her.

"We're all hungry," Uncle John tried to joke.

"We'll be along in a little bit," Mandie said and then, remembering their arrangements, she added, as she tried to smile, "Orphans and all. Aunt Lou and Jenny have already prepared dinner enough for everyone, and we want to eat together."

Elizabeth glanced at Uncle John, and he said, "Of course, just hurry up and bring everyone over. We're starving." He, Elizabeth, and the Woodards left.

Mandie helped re-dress the children after the others were gone. Mrs. Taft had stayed to see what she could do. She helped Aunt Lou and Jenny herd the children across the road to the house. Liza went along to control them.

Left alone with Joe and Uncle Ned, Mandie said, "I'm sorry everything went so badly. I guess I ruined it all."

Joe clasped her hand and said, "No, you didn't, Mandie. You did wonderful. It was that selfish man who tried to ruin everything. I'm going on to the house because I know you want to talk with Uncle Ned. You haven't seen him since he got here. But like your Uncle

66

John said, please hurry. I'm hungry!" He laughed as he left.

"Uncle Ned, what did I do wrong?" Mandie asked when they were alone. They sat down on a low bench.

"Papoose, must learn to think," Uncle Ned told her. "I always say, think before acting. Think what people will say when Papoose demand money and work from them."

Mandie looked at him in surprise. "But I didn't demand it, Uncle Ned. I was only asking for it," she said.

"No, no, Papoose must walk softly when asking for something," he tried to explain. "Cannot make people do things. Must set example to influence them."

"I thought I was doing the right thing, showing them the orphans and telling them about the house," Mandie said.

"Papoose must set example. Show people she can work and give," the old man kept trying to explain.

"You mean we should go ahead and start work on the house if Mr. Simpson will let us?"

Uncle Ned smiled and said, "Yes, begin work. Others will come."

"I don't know. The other people in the audience were saying things that sounded like they were agreeing with what the man said," Mandie insisted.

"Trust," Uncle Ned said. "Work. Other people will work."

"Trust, yes, I must trust in the Lord to help," Mandie agreed.

As the old man and the young girl held hands, they looked above and said a prayer.

"Dear Lord, we need help to help the little orphans,

please. Thank you, dear Lord," Mandie said.

"Yes, Big God, please help," Uncle Ned added as he also prayed.

Uncle Ned stood up and said, "Must go eat now."

Mandie laughed as she wiped her reddened eyes and said, "Even you are hungry."

At the house Mandie discussed her decision with the others, and everyone agreed to pitch in and help if Mr. Simpson would allow them to do so. And Mrs. Taft offered whatever money was needed to get things going.

Mandie's mother insisted on opening up rooms on the third floor of the house for the orphans to use until they could be returned to the places they lived or until they could get their own home. Liza was given complete care of them and she was excited with the responsibility.

❄   ❄   ❄

When Christmas Eve came, everyone went out caroling, orphans and all, except for Mrs. Taft, who insisted she wanted to stay home. But she did join them later at the church for the Christmas Eve service. A local retired minister took the pulpit to deliver the sermon.

Mandie looked around and realized the church was full. She wondered if Mr. Simpson had returned yet. Then she happened to see him all the way across the sanctuary. He seemed to know the man beside him and she wondered who that person could be.

During the service she could only think of what Uncle Ned had said. She must show an example for the people to follow. Did that include standing up to apologize for what she had said at the play? Passages in the Bible ran through her mind—the one about not letting the sun go down upon your wrath, about forgiving one another, about returning good for evil, and many more. And she made her decision.

As soon as the minister closed the sermon, she quickly slipped out of her seat, raced up to the pulpit, and blurted out her apologies as the pastor looked at her in surprise.

"I want to apologize to all of you, every one of you, for the way I made the request for help Sunday at the play," she began, jumbling words as they left her mouth. "I know I was wrong to demand anything from you good people, and I want to ask your forgiveness for letting my temper out. I am sorry. Please forgive me." Her knees almost folded and she rushed back to her seat.

Uncle Ned, sitting beside her, smiled as she sat down.

The people in the church all began murmuring and Mandie wondered if someone were going to blast out at her again. Then suddenly the man who had started it all appeared at the pulpit and began talking loudly, "I must ask your forgiveness, Miss Amanda Shaw. I am sorry from the bottom of my heart for my outburst. You were trying to do a wonderful thing and I was trying to stop you. I am sorry. And to show I mean it, I have the first hundred dollars right here to begin work on the house, and I will do any job that I am capable of doing to help get things going." He waved the money in the air.

Mandie, with tears flowing down her face, once again ran back up to the stage to shake the man's hand.

The audience became noisy as they pushed their way to the front to give money and to offer labor on the house.

Suddenly the piano blasted loudly over the uproar as the old hymn, "Count Your Blessings," quieted shouts from the crowd and stirred them into loud singing.

Mandie looked down and saw Joe pounding away on the piano. He looked at her and grinned.

Everything was working out. The Lord had answered their prayers. Mandie found Uncle Ned at her side and together they looked upward and said, "Thank you, dear Lord."

❋ ❋ ❋

THE END

Mandie and Joe's Christmas Secret

A Drama in Three Acts

by Lois Gladys Leppard

TIME: 1901

PLACE: Franklin, North Carolina

ACT I: Scene 1 – The Sunday school room in a
                     church basement.
                     Late afternoon in December.
           Scene 2 – The Sunday school room in a
                     church basement.
                     One evening several days
                     later.

ACT II: Sanctuary of church.
           Sunday morning, three days before
           Christmas.

ACT III: Sanctuary of church.
           Christmas Eve night.

CHARACTERS
(in order of appearance)

Mandie (Amanda) Shaw, 13-year-old blond girl
Joe Woodard, 15-year-old boy
2 small orphan girls
2 small orphan boys
Mrs. Taft, Mandie's grandmother
Liza, the maid in Mandie's house
4 additional orphan girls
2 additional orphan boys

George Simpson, New York actor
People in audience of church
Jenny, cook at Mandie's house, as Mary
Abraham, yardman at Mandie's house, as Joseph
Uncle Ned, elderly Cherokee Indian
Man who speaks out in church
Local retired minister, elderly

ACT I — Scene 1

THE SCENE: *The Sunday school room in the basement of a church. The room is long, with a window at left downstage and an outside door next to it. Shrubbery can be seen through the window. Wooden chairs and benches are lined up facing a small table at right upstage. A hallway goes offstage beyond the table. A few toys are in a large basket sitting in the corner of the room near the hallway exit. It is late afternoon in December. There is a fire going in the heater left upstage.*

AT CURTAIN: *The stage is empty. The door opens. Mandie, wearing a cloak with a hood, enters as she pushes two little girls in ahead of her. Joe, with two little boys, enters right behind her.*

MANDIE

(Hastily removing the girls' coats and bonnets and tossing them on a chair as the girls race for the toys.)

We need more. I was hoping we could locate at least a dozen.

JOE

(*Picking up the boys' coats and hats as the boys throw them off and race to join the girls at the toys.*)

It's going to be hard, if not impossible, to find eight more, especially with Christmas so close.

(*He sits on a bench nearby.*)

MANDIE

(*Pushing back the hood on her cloak and sitting down beside Joe.*)

But we've just got to do it. I want this Christmas, in this year of 1901, to be remembered as a *real* Christmas with all its true meaning, and this is the way we planned to do it.

JOE

We might could try something else.

MANDIE

But this was the only idea we could come up with.

(*Rising, she takes off her cloak and hangs it and the children's clothes on pegs on the wall upstage and walks over to the heater.*)

We need to build up this fire and get the children warm, don't you think?

JOE

I'll take care of it.

> (*He hurries offstage through the hallway exit and quickly returns with an armload of wood, which he places by the heater. Opening the heater door, he adds a piece of wood to the fire. Closes door.*)

MANDIE

> (*Watching.*)

That ought to warm this place up.

JOE

> (*Dusting off his hands as he straightens up.*)

How are we going to do everything that is necessary, just the two of us? I think we need someone to help us, maybe Liza?

MANDIE

I'm not sure we can trust Liza. I know she wouldn't deliberately give away our secret, but she might just forget and say something to somebody. Besides, what would the other servants say if Liza just disappeared now and then and didn't do her work?

JOE

Well, who else is there?

MANDIE

There's my mother and there's Uncle John, but I don't want them to know what we're doing. What we really need is a wagon so we could go farther out into the country.

JOE

A wagon? The only wagon we'd have a chance of getting belongs to your Uncle John. When my father and mother get here, I'm sure they'll be in the buggy.

MANDIE

I sure am glad y'all are spending the holidays with us. I couldn't do all this by myself.

(*She looks up at Joe and smiles.*)

JOE

(*Running his fingers through his hair.*)

And I don't think you and I together can do all this. Mandie, we need someone else in on this. For instance, how are we going to take care of these children down here in the church basement? They have to be fed and will need supervision. We can't just go off and leave them in here all alone.

MANDIE

(*Walking about the room and glancing at the children playing.*)

I know that, Joe. One of us can stay here while the other one goes to find more. And I'm sure I can get plenty of food from our kitchen. After all, I live just across the road. And we've got that stack of shuck mattresses in the other room for them to sleep on, plus all those quilts I found in our linen closet. So I don't see any problem with anything.

JOE

(*Strolling over to look out the window.*)

It's an awfully big job for just the two of us.

MANDIE

(*Walking over to the window.*)

Look! It's beginning to snow.

(*Snowflakes can be seen falling on the shrub-bery outside the window.*)

JOE

Yes, and I think we'd better get some food in here for the night.

MANDIE

All right. It's not quite time for Jenny to begin preparing supper at our house, so while there's no one in our kitchen, I'll make a quick trip over there and bring back whatever I can find.

(*She walks over to the clothes hanging on the pegs upstage, takes down her cloak, and quickly puts it on.*)

JOE

(*Turning around to watch Mandie.*)

Thank goodness you don't have a pastor at this church right now, or he'd be sure to catch up with us.

MANDIE

(*Walking to the door.*)

The new one won't arrive until February. I'll be right back.

(*Mandie opens the door.*)

Grandmother!

(*Mandie steps back into the room.*)

(*Mrs. Taft enters through the door. She is expensively dressed in winter clothes.*)

MRS. TAFT

Mr. Bond brought me from the depot, and he told me you were probably over here getting a play ready for the holidays.

(*She looks around the room, sees the four children.*)

MANDIE

You're a day early.

MRS. TAFT

Amanda, whose children are these?

MANDIE

(*Mandie glances at Joe, who stands listening.*)

Grandmother, they are a secret. And we need some help.

MRS. TAFT

Help, dear? What kind of help?

(*Mandie glances at Joe again.*)

MANDIE

Well, all kinds of help. But, please understand, Grandmother, what I'm about to tell you is a secret, and you won't give away my secret, will you?

MRS. TAFT

Amanda, what on earth are you talking about? I've got to get on across the road to your house. Mr. Bond will be taking in my luggage, and your mother is going to wonder where I am.

MANDIE

Well, you see, Joe Woodard and I have determined that we will make this Christmas a real Christmas, the way Jesus' birth ought to be celebrated. And we've made these secret plans, but we need some help. We don't want anyone to know what we're doing so it will be a big surprise.

MRS. TAFT

(*Looking from Mandie to Joe and back.*)

Amanda, what are you and Joe up to? Please hurry and explain.

MANDIE

We are collecting orphans to put on a Christmas play here at the church. We got permission to give a play since we don't have a pastor right now, but nobody knows how we are planning on doing this. And there are so many angles and odds and ends to this, and only two of us to get it all done. We need someone in on our secret, and I think you are the best secret-keeper I know of.

(*She grins at Mrs. Taft.*)

MRS. TAFT

Oh, dear! And where are you getting all these orphans?

(*She looks at Joe.*)

JOE

Mandie is in charge.

(*He grins.*)

MANDIE

We just brought two little girls from the Swafford farm and two boys from the Pinsons down on Bryson City Road. And we are looking for more. We need about twelve to sing in the play. But now that we've begun all this, I can see that we need someone to help. Will you, Grandmother, will you, please?

(*She looks at her grandmother anxiously.*)

MRS. TAFT

Do you mean to say these people just let you take the children off like that?

MANDIE

They're orphans, Grandmother. It seems nobody cares about orphans—where they go, or what they do. That's why we decided to have no one but orphans in our play. We want everybody to change their attitude toward these little children without mothers and fathers.

MRS. TAFT

(*Watching the children playing in the corner.*)

Amanda, I know you're always trying to do good, but

sometimes you have some strange ideas about how to accomplish things.

(*She sighs.*)

What is it you want me to do, dear?

MANDIE

(*Smiling.*)

Oh, thank you, Grandmother, for understanding. Here's what we need. First of all, we need some money to buy wood for the heaters, the one in here and the one in the sanctuary. We need food for the children, and some of them just have to have warmer clothes. And we need a wagon, so we can go on out into the country and find more orphaned children—

MRS. TAFT

(*Interrupting.*)

All right, all right. Please tell me quickly what you want me to do.

MANDIE

(*Glancing at Joe.*)

Joe and I are hoping the people here in Franklin will join with us in helping the orphans, but we also need someone to help us with the work.

MRS. TAFT

And just how do you think this play and whatever else you do will help the orphan situation?

MANDIE

After the play is over, we are going to ask the audience to make a contribution toward the support of the orphans.

(She quickly looks at Mrs. Taft.)

Did you know that people give orphans a home in order to get free labor? These tiny children who don't have a place to live are farmed out to anyone who is willing to give them a place to stay in exchange for work. Imagine these small children having to work for their living!

MRS. TAFT

It is a sorry situation right now, Amanda. I agree on that. But it will take a lot to make a difference.

(She looks at Mandie.)

And you said you need help with this. Have you spoken to your father's old Cherokee friend, Uncle Ned, about what you're doing? Maybe he could help.

MANDIE

I haven't seen Uncle Ned since Joe and I decided to do this. We've had to act so fast. Christmas is just around the corner, you know.

MRS. TAFT

Of course I'll be glad to give you whatever money y'all need, but I think you should ask Liza to help out with this. She would be really good at taking care of the children.

MANDIE

I'm not sure she can keep a secret. Maybe you could explain to her that no one else is to know what we're doing. She would listen to you.

MRS. TAFT

I'll see what I can do, but right now I must be getting over to the house, or someone will come looking for me.

MANDIE

I'll go with you, Grandmother. I have to get food from our kitchen for the children's supper.

(*She turns to Joe.*)

Joe, I'll be right back.

(*Mandie and Mrs. Taft walk toward the door.*)

(*The door opens. Liza, the Shaw maid, enters.*)

LIZA

(*Closing the door.*)

Miz Taft, Mistuh Bond he told me to come and git you. Miz 'Lizabeth seen you come over heah.

MRS. TAFT

You came at just the right time, Liza. We need your help. Amanda has these children (*She motions toward the children.*) staying here in the basement of the church, and we would like you to watch them while Amanda and Joe eat supper since you won't be having your meal until later.

LIZA

(*Looking at the children in surprise.*)

Chillun in de church?

(*She looks at Mrs. Taft.*)

But, Aunt Lou, whut she gwine say if I run off like dat?

MRS. TAFT

(*With her hand on the doorknob.*)

I'll explain to her. Now, Amanda, you and Joe hurry on over to the house.

(*She exits the door, closing it behind her.*)

JOE

We won't be gone real long, Liza. We'll be back in plenty of time for you to go have your supper.

LIZA

(*Looking at the children.*)

Where you git dese heah chillun? Who dey be?

MANDIE

They're orphans. Just like you. They don't have a mother or father. We need you to watch them to be sure

they don't get too close to the heater and they don't go outside.

LIZA

Dem po' lil' chillun, no mamas and no papas.

MANDIE

And I forgot to tell you, Liza, but we need you to stay here with them tonight.

LIZA

You means spend de night in dis heah spooky church?

(*Her eyes widen.*)

MANDIE

Liza, this church is not spooky. It's God's house.

LIZA

But I cain't see God. How does I knows He be heah? S'pose de Devil he be heah, too?

MANDIE

Oh, Liza, the Devil wouldn't dare come into God's house. Remember, these little children need you. They don't have any mothers and fathers.

LIZA

(*Glancing at the children and then looking back at Mandie.*)

But, Missy 'Manda, I'se jes' plain skeered to stay in dis heah place all night 'less y'all stays, too.

(*She glances toward the window.*)

And all dem dead people out dere in de graveyard.

JOE

I tell you what, Liza. As soon as everyone in the house goes to bed I'll come back over here and sleep in the next room if you'll stay in here with the children.

LIZA

(*Slowly replying.*)

Well, I s'pose me and dese heah chillun be all right if you sleeps in de next room.

(*She adds quickly.*)

But mind you now, if I wakes up and you done gwine left dis heah place, den I be leavin', too.

MANDIE

And I'll come and stay any time Joe is not here. We won't leave you alone all night. Now we've got to get some food for the children's supper and we'll be right back.

LIZA

I guess dat's all right den.

(*She walks over to watch the children.*)

JOE

(*Putting on his cap and opening the door.*)

We won't be gone long.

(*He waits for Mandie to step outside ahead of him.*)

MANDIE

(*Going out the door.*)

We can rotate nights, Joe. I can stay tonight, and you tomorrow night, and so on.

JOE

(*Following Mandie out the door.*)

That's fine.

CURTAIN

ACT I - Scene 2

THE SCENE: *Several days later in the Sunday school room in the basement of the church. A stack of papers is on the table. It is evening, and only the light of the moon can be seen through the window. Several costumes are lying here and there on chairs and on the table. Two kerosene lamps are lit, one at each end of the room.*

AT CURTAIN: *The four children from Scene 1 are on stage, plus four more girls and two more boys. Liza is playing with the children at the end of the room right upstage. Mandie and Joe are examining the costumes.*

MANDIE

(*Holding up a small, white robe.*)

Aunt Lou certainly did a good job on these. I've got to tell her how much I appreciate her work.

JOE

(*Holding a pair of wings to go on the robe.*)

She certainly did. We're lucky your grandmother came

to our rescue. Without your cook, Jenny, preparing food for the children and Aunt Lou making the costumes, we would never in this world get finished on time.

MANDIE

You're right.

(*She puts the costume down on the table and looks at the children.*)

You know, anybody could look at Jasper and Jake and tell they were brothers, but the boys themselves don't seem aware of it. It's a shame they've been put into different homes since they were babies. I imagine this is the first time they've ever really seen each other.

JOE

(*Also looking at the children.*)

I think we ought to tell them they're brothers.

MANDIE

I don't imagine Mrs. Oglesby, who keeps Jake, would mind. But that bunch of bootleggers who have Jasper would probably raise the roof.

JOE

There's nothing they could do about it if we did tell the boys. In fact, Jasper might be taken away from them if the right people knew what kind of home he is in.

MANDIE

But, Joe, think how it would hurt the boys to know they were brothers and couldn't live together.

JOE

(*Pacing the floor.*)

This thing has become too complicated for comfort.

MANDIE

It's not much longer to wait. Sunday we'll give the play, and Grandmother has already promised we could all go Christmas caroling on Christmas Eve, and keep the children here until late Christmas Day on Wednesday so we can give them the presents she is going to place beneath the tree.

JOE

Don't you think we'd better practice a little more for the play? The children need to learn to stay together on the songs.

MANDIE

All right.

(*She looks over at Liza.*)

Liza, let's line the children up and sing some of the songs. The more they practice, the better they'll be.

LIZA

(*Getting up off the floor where she has been sitting with the children and urging the ten children to line up.*)

Let's stand up straight heah down by de table and show Missy 'Manda how good we is. How 'bout dat "Silent Night" song we done learned?

(*All ten children obey as they line up and begin singing.*)

Silent Night, Holy Night—loud now so Mistuh Joe he kin hear you, too.

(*Mandie and Joe stand nearby to watch and listen as the children go through the whole song without a noticeable mistake.*)

MANDIE

(*Claps as the song ends.*) (*The children go back to play.*)

That was wonderful!

(*Turning to Joe.*)

They need some music. I didn't even think about that. And I don't know where we're going to get someone to play the piano.

JOE

(*Walking toward the hallway exit.*)

There's a piano in this next room here.

(*He exits.*)

MANDIE

(*Remains on stage.*)

Yes, but what good is it to us?

(*Suddenly the sound of "Silent Night, Holy Night," bursts forth from the piano in the next room.*)

MANDIE

(*Hurrying to the hallway exit. She looks offstage as she calls to Joe.*)

Joe Woodard!

(*The music stops.*)

When did you learn to play the piano?

JOE

(*Entering from the hallway exit.*)

A long, long time ago.

MANDIE

I've known you all my life, and I didn't know you could play the piano. Why have you been so secretive about it?

JOE

(*Flopping into a chair near the table.*)

I haven't been. My mother taught me as soon as I could walk, just about. But I revolted after I got up in school.

MANDIE

I'm glad to find this out about you, because I'm sure we're going to make use of your talent for this play.

(*She grins at him.*)

JOE

(*Stands up and yawns, picks up his coat and cap from a chair.*)

I think I'm going to the house now. It's late.

MANDIE

(*Stands up.*)

I know. The children have stayed up way past their bedtime.

JOE

(*Placing his coat and cap back on the chair.*)

I'll stoke up the fire in the heater for you and get the mattresses ready for the children.

(*He goes to the heater, opens the door, pokes at the fire inside, and adds more wood from a pile on the floor.*)

MANDIE

Liza, it's bedtime. Take the girls to the other room and get them dressed for bed. Joe and I will make up the mattresses, and then you can help the boys.

LIZA

(*Stands up and motions to the girls.*)

Come on, all you lil' gals. Bedtime.

(*The girls follow her as she exits off the hallway.*)

JOE

I'll get the mattresses.

(*He starts toward the exit off the hallway.*)

We put them in the big closet down the hall this morning.

(*Exits.*)

MANDIE

(*Follows him across the stage.*)

I'll help you.

(*Exits off the hallway.*)

LIZA

(*Enters from the hallway, gently pushing the little girls ahead of her. The children are wearing their nightclothes.*)

Come on, you lil' boys. You's next.

(*Mandie and Joe enter carrying a cornshuck*

mattress, which they place on two benches they push together.)

(Liza exits through the hallway as she herds the boys ahead of her.)

JOE

(Straightening up.)

One down. Four to go.

MANDIE

(Giving the mattress a little pat.)

Five to go. Don't forget Liza has to have a bed, too.

JOE

I thought some of the little ones could sleep three on one mattress. With the backs of benches to keep them from falling off, there's plenty of room.

MANDIE

(Straightening up.)

You're right. And I'll sleep in the next room.

(Mandie and Joe exit through the hallway and bring in more mattresses. Liza leads the little boys back into the room in their nightclothes and puts them and the girls on their beds. Then she helps Mandie and Joe and gets her own mat-

tress, which she places on the floor between the boys and girls.)

MANDIE

Liza and I can get the quilts. You go ahead. See you in the morning.

JOE

(Picks up his coat and hat, puts them on.)

Good-night.

(He goes to the open door.)

MANDIE

Good-night.

(Joe exits through the doorway and closes the door.)
(Liza exits through the hallway and comes back with an armload of quilts, which she lays on the table.)

LIZA

I git de rest of dem quilts if you wants to kivver de chil-lun wid dese.

(Exits.)

MANDIE

Sure, Liza.

> (*She begins going from bed to bed distributing the covers.*)

LIZA

> (*Enters from the hallway with more quilts.*)

Dis be all of dem. I left one fo' you.

> (*Mandie takes some of the quilts, and she and Liza finish distributing them. The children are all covered for the night.*)

MANDIE

You go ahead to bed, Liza. I'm going to sit down at the far end and go over the script for the play one more time before I retire for the night.

> (*She picks up the stack of papers on the table.*)

LIZA

> (*Flopping down on her mattress and pulling a quilt over her.*)

'Night, Missy 'Manda.

MANDIE

> (*She walks over to the lamp at the hallway end of the room and blows out the light.*)

Good-night, Liza.

(She carries the papers and goes to sit down in a chair by the other lamp, which is near the door.)

(The scene becomes quiet. There is a giggle now and then from the children, but they soon fall asleep.)

(Mandie reads her papers and begins to nod. She drops off to sleep in the chair. She is suddenly awakened by someone (George) opening the door.)

MANDIE

(Quickly sitting up and rubbing her eyes. She looks toward the door.)

Who is it?

George

(Pausing just inside the doorway as he closes the door.)

I'm sorry. I didn't know someone was using the basement. You see, I've just got back into town after many long years away, and I thought I'd run over to visit this old church where I went as a child.

MANDIE

(Gasping as she quickly stands up and straightens her skirts.)

I see. My name is Amanda Shaw, Mandie for short, and these children are all orphans.

(*She waves her hand toward the sleeping children.*)

GEORGE

I apologize. I'm George Simpson. Are you related to Mr. John Shaw?

MANDIE

(*Completely awake now, responds in surprise.*)

Yes, he's my uncle, and he married my mother after my father, Jim Shaw, died.

GEORGE

(*With a big smile.*)

Well, well, well! I remember your father very well before he married your mother. After that he seemed to disappear, but Mr. John Shaw was very kind to me when I was growing up. You see, I was an orphan, too.

MANDIE

If you were an orphan, where did you live here in Franklin when you attended this church?

GEORGE

Oh, here and there, mostly with my mother's old cousins, who have just died. That's why I'm back in town.

MANDIE

Did I know them? Who were they?

GEORGE

No, you probably didn't know them, because they left town years ago to live over in Jackson County. They owned the huge house on the hill just as you go around the curve on Bryson City Road. It has been closed up ever since they moved away, and I find it's in bad shape. I'm their only heir, and they left it to me, but I don't know what I'll be doing with it.

MANDIE

Don't you want to live in it? I know the house you're talking about. It looks like a mansion, really, it's so big.

GEORGE

No, it would be impossible for me to live here in Franklin. You see, I have a home in New York and my business is up there, so I don't need the house.

MANDIE

New York? I've never been there, but some day I will go. Couldn't you move your business down here so you could live in the house? I'm sure it would be beautiful if someone would fix it up.

GEORGE

(*Laughing.*)

No, I couldn't do that. I'm an actor and I have to stay where the theater is.

MANDIE

(*Quickly looking at George.*)

The children are here temporarily so we can have them in a Christmas play here in the church. My friend Joe Woodard and I are presenting it the Sunday before Christmas—next Sunday, in fact.

(*Looking up directly into his eyes.*)

Could we persuade you to act in our play? Please?

GEORGE

Sorry, but I won't be in Franklin this coming weekend. I will return next week to do something about the house though.

MANDIE

How much are you going to sell the house for? I mean, you must be planning to sell it since you don't want it.

GEORGE

Why? Do you know of someone who might be interested in buying it?

MANDIE

(*Sighing.*)

No, not exactly. I was just thinking what a perfect home it would make for these orphans here. You see, they've all been farmed out wherever a family needs them to do work, and I'm sure they're being mistreated. Can you imagine little ones like these having to work for their keep?

GEORGE

(*Pacing about a few steps.*)

Yes, I know exactly what it's like. I went through all that and somehow managed to survive. I ran away from the last place that gave me a home, because they beat me. I was fourteen and I hitchhiked—walked most of the way, really—to New York. I got various backbreaking jobs and was able to get some education. Then, when I was seventeen, I was really lucky. I got a job as driver for one of the big Broadway producers. He gave me my start in show business. But I am well aware that not all orphans are given an opportunity like that.

MANDIE

(*Smiling.*)

I'm sorry, Mr. Simpson, but I am happy for you now.

(*Smiling, she looks up at him.*)

Don't you think the house would be a good place to put these orphans?

GEORGE

(*Pauses for a moment before replying.*)

Yes, I agree. I remember being in the house. It probably

has twenty rooms. But it's in bad shape right now.

(*Mandie frowns and walks around.*)

MANDIE

(*Stops to face George.*)

I know what we could do! If you would give us the house for the orphans, I could probably get the money from the townspeople to fix it up.

GEORGE

But what about maintenance? How would you run the operation? After all, there are regular bills, such as food and clothing among other things, that have to be funded from somewhere.

MANDIE

(*Closing her eyes as she looks upward. Then turns to look at George.*)

If you will donate the house to the orphans, I will come up with the money to run it. I have faith in the people's kindness here in Franklin and, above all, I have faith that God will supply the funds.

(*She clasps her hands as she holds her breath, waiting for his answer.*)

GEORGE

(*Hesitates a moment. Steps forward with his hand out.*)

It's a deal. You get the money rounded up and I will be back in town, probably on Christmas Eve. We'll seal the bargain then.

(*They shake hands.*)

MANDIE

(*Suddenly stands on tiptoe and plants a kiss on George's cheek.*)

Thank you! With all my heart, I thank you!

GEORGE

(*Quickly embraces her and then steps back.*)

Now I have to go. I have someone waiting for me. I will see you as soon as I get back in town.

(*He walks toward the door.*)

MANDIE

(*Follows George to door.*)

Thank you again.

GEORGE

Good-night now.

(*He exits the door.*)

MANDIE

(*She closes the door and leans against it.*)

(*Softly to herself.*)

It's going to be a long night before morning comes when I can tell Joe the good news. The Lord is going to take care of His orphans.

CURTAIN

ACT II

THE SCENE: *The sanctuary of the church seen from a side view. The platform stage is left stage with church pews lined up in front of it and going out of sight at right stage. The stage has a large decorated Christmas tree at the rear with more decorations here and there. There is a chair near the front of the platform stage. Wrapped gifts are piled high under and around the tree. It is Sunday morning, three days before Christmas. A manger is at left downstage, with straw and a rough bed for the baby Jesus.*

AT CURTAIN: *Mandie, dressed in a long, red dress, with a bunch of holly with red berries pinned to her shoulder, and her hair hanging loose down her back, is sitting in the chair with a book in her hands. There is a lighted lamp next to her. The rest of the stage is dark. Joe is playing soft music on the piano offstage. The pews are filled with people.*

MANDIE

(Reading from the book as she sits in the chair.)

Joseph and Mary went from Galilee, out of the city of Nazareth into Judea, and into the city of David, which is called Bethlehem, to be taxed according to a law made by Caesar Augustus. He declared that all the world should be taxed. While they were there they had to stay in a stable, because there was no room for them in the inn.

(A light illuminates the manger left downstage. Mary and Joseph are sitting by the manger in the straw.)

MANDIE

(Continues reading.)

Mary's first son was born in that stable manger. She wrapped Him in swaddling clothes and laid Him in the rough bed.

(As she reads this, Mary picks up a baby from the manger for the audience to see and carefully places Him back in the bed. He is wrapped in white garments.)

MANDIE

(Continues reading.)

There were shepherds watching their flocks in the

fields. The Lord's angels appeared to them and they were afraid. The angel said—

JOE

(*From offstage.*)

Fear not; behold, I bring you good tidings of a great joy, which shall be to all people. For unto you is born this day in the city of David, a Savior, which is Christ the Lord. And this shall be a sign unto you. Ye shall find the babe wrapped in swaddling clothes, lying in a manger.

> (*Liza, with the ten orphans dressed in white robes and wings, enters left stage and comes to stand behind the manger.*)

LIZA AND THE ORPHANS

Glory to God in the highest, and on earth peace, good will toward men.

MANDIE

(*Continues reading.*)

And the shepherds came to see what had come to pass, and after they had seen the baby Jesus, they went out into the night and spread the word. Herod, the king, sent wise men from the east to find the newborn baby. The star they saw in the east went along with them and showed them the way.

> (*Pause for soft music from offstage.*)

MANDIE

(Continues reading.)

When the wise men saw the baby, they fell down on their knees and worshipped Him. They brought gold, frankincense, and myrrh and laid it before Him. But God warned them they should not return to Herod and that they should return to their country by another route. And after they left, the Lord's angel appeared to Joseph in a dream telling him to arise and take the baby and His mother and flee into Egypt, because Herod would seek out the baby and try to kill Him. Then Herod died.

LIZA AND THE ORPHANS

And because the son of Herod was king now, Joseph didn't go to Israel like God told him. He went to Galilee instead, and settled down in the city called Nazareth.

MANDIE

(Closing the book and rising.)

And today we are having an early celebration of Jesus' birth.

(She turns to look at Liza. Liza herds the orphans forward to stand in a line across the stage.)

(The piano offstage begins playing, and Mandie steps to one side as the orphans, led by Liza, begin to sing old Christmas songs.)

(After two songs, Mandie waves to Liza to stop.

The piano music also stops. Mandie steps forward to center downstage.)

MANDIE

Ladies and gentlemen, I'd like you to meet our chorus. (*She motions toward the orphans, and they all come to stand by her.*) These ten little children are all orphans. I doubt that any of you knows any of these little tykes. When Joe Woodard and I got permission to put on this play at the church, we wanted to make this a real Christmas—what Christmas really stands for—Jesus' birthday, not just the time when Santa Claus comes and everyone is so anxious to receive all the gifts they can get, with no mention of our Savior. Presents should be given to show our love for other people, people who are poor and needy and who won't receive much else for Christmas.

(*Mandie pauses as she spots Uncle Ned in the audience.*)

These children don't have a real home. They live wherever people will take them in exchange for work. Imagine little ones like these having to work for their keep.

(*She pauses as a murmur goes up from the audience.*)

(*Continuing.*)

I want to ask each and every one of you to help these orphans. And I'll tell you how you can do it. You probably all know about the old house that's been closed up for years and years out on Bryson City Road, just around the curve. Well, the owners died recently in Jackson County, where they had moved many years ago. And I met the man who has inherited the house, George Simpson, their cousin.

(*She pauses as she sees some of the older people looking at each other in recognition of the name.*)

(*She takes a deep breath and continues.*)

Now, Mr. Simpson has agreed to give us the house for a home for these orphans *provided* we donate enough time, work, and money to get it in livable shape and maintain it.

(*She pauses as there are loud murmurs from the audience.*)

MANDIE

(*Continuing as she looks over the audience.*)

Just look at these two little boys here, Jake and Jasper. (*She motions toward the two boys.*) They are not aware of it yet, but they were separated when they were babies after the death of their parents. That shouldn't ever happen to anyone.

(*She pauses to allow the audience to make remarks among themselves.*)

(*The two boys step out of line to look at each other and rush to embrace.*)

(*Continuing in a stern voice.*)

116

Now here's what every person in this audience *must* do. Everybody here can give something. If you don't have money to give, you can give time and work. We have promised Mr. Simpson that the people of Franklin will come to the rescue of these little orphans, and we are going to keep our promise. Please don't say you're too busy or you can't afford to give even a few dollars. No matter how poor you are, you can still share in some way. We can always find someone poorer than we are, and these little orphans are poorer than anyone in this audience.

(*She pauses, but the audience is quiet.*)

(*Continuing in a firm voice.*)

Now, I want the donations to begin. Who will make the first one? We have a chance to help these children, and I want you to assist in some way. Come on now. Who has money to give? Who will volunteer to work on the house? Speak up.

(*The audience has become restless and murmurs among themselves.*)

MAN

(*Stands up, shaking his fist and yelling at Mandie.*)

We don't need no half-breed telling us what to do with our money and time! Who do you think you are?

MANDIE

(*Shocked.*)

I am what God made me and I can't change that so you'd better like it!

JOE

(*Rushing out from behind the curtain to Mandie's side. Yelling and shaking his fist in the air.*)

This is God's house and no place for such talk, mister!

UNCLE NED

(*Rushing up on the stage to join Mandie.*)

Come, Papoose.

AUDIENCE

No, we don't! No! Never! Use your own money!

(*The audience quickly exit the church.*)

MRS. TAFT

(*Rushing up on the stage to join Mandie.*)

I'll fix that man! You just wait and see! He'll live to regret what he said to my granddaughter!

MANDIE

(*Seeing Liza and the orphans standing nearby.*)

Please take off their costumes, Liza, and take the children all over to the house. We're going to eat there.

(*She wipes her eyes with the back of her hand.*)

(*Liza exits with the orphans, and Jenny and Abraham, who played Joseph and Mary, follow them offstage.*)

MRS. TAFT

Come on, dear. Everyone is due over at your house in a few minutes. Your mother and Uncle John went on ahead, before that ugly man made his remarks, and asked me to see that everyone else gets there on time.

MANDIE

Just give me a few minutes, please, Grandmother, and I'll be along.

MRS. TAFT

All right now. Don't be too long.

(*She exits the way Liza went.*)

(*Mandie steps down from the stage and sits down in the front pew. Joe and Uncle Ned follow her.*)

MANDIE

(*Looking at Joe.*)

I'm sorry everything went so badly. I guess I ruined it all.

JOE

(*Reaching to hold her hand.*)

No, you didn't, Mandie. You did wonderful. It was that selfish man who tried to ruin everything.

(*He stands up.*)

I'm going on over to your house because I know you want to talk with Uncle Ned. You haven't seen him since he got here. But please hurry. I'm hungry.

(*He laughs as he exits left stage.*)

MANDIE

Uncle Ned, what did I do wrong?

UNCLE NED

Papoose must learn to think. I always say think. Think before acting. Think what people will say when Papoose demand money and work from them.

MANDIE

(*Looking at him in surprise.*)

But I didn't demand it, Uncle Ned. I was only asking for it.

UNCLE NED

No, no, Papoose must walk softly when asking for something. Cannot *make* people do things. Must set example to influence them.

MANDIE

But I thought I was doing the right thing showing them the orphans and telling them about the house.

UNCLE NED

Papoose must set example. Show people she can work and give.

MANDIE

You mean we should go ahead and start work on the house if Mr. Simpson will let us?

UNCLE NED

(*Smiling.*)

Yes, begin work. Others will come.

MANDIE

I'm not sure about that. The other people in the audience were saying things that sounded like they were agreeing with what the man said.

UNCLE NED

Trust. We work. Other people will work.

MANDIE

Trust, yes, I must trust in the Lord to help.

(*Mandie reaches for the old Indian's hand, and together they look upward to say a prayer.*)

MANDIE

Dear Lord, we need your help to provide a home for the little orphans. Please help. Thank you, dear Lord.

UNCLE NED

Yes, Big God, we need help. Please help.

(*Uncle Ned stands and pulls Mandie to her feet.*)

Must go eat now.

MANDIE

(*Wiping her reddened eyes with the back of her hand.*)

Even you are hungry!

(*She smiles up at him as they start to exit the stage.*)

CURTAIN

ACT III

THE SCENE: *The sanctuary of the church seen from a side view, as in Act II, but there is a pulpit and a small table below it where several collection plates sit. It is Christmas Eve night.*

AT CURTAIN: *A local retired minister is standing before the pulpit. Mandie, Uncle Ned, Joe, Liza, and the orphans are all sitting on the front rows of the pews. All seats are occupied, and people are standing in the aisles.*

MINISTER

We should remember that Christmas is the celebration of Jesus' birth, and not only an occasion for receiving gifts. We should be giving gifts to those less fortunate than we are—the poor, the disabled, and of course the orphans such as you have had here in the play on Sunday.

(*An amen comes from the Amen Corner in the back of the church.*)

(Minister continues.)

Christmas should be a time of forgiving. Don't let the sun go down on your wrath. You may not be here tomorrow to ask the other person's forgiveness. And the sum of the commandments is that we love one another. If you really want to get even with someone you think has done you wrong, forgive that person and be nice to him or her. That person will be at a loss as to what to do next and, most of the time, amends can be made. Now let's stand and sing our final hymn tonight, the old Christmas carol "O Holy Night." Let's all join in.

(The audience stands and sings the song.)

(As soon as the song is over, Mandie rushes up to the pulpit. The minister looks at her in surprise.)

MANDIE

(Speaking to the minister.)

Please excuse me, but I have something to say before everyone leaves.

MINISTER

Yes, miss, go right ahead.

(He steps back from the pulpit as Mandie steps up to it.)

MANDIE

(*Looking over the audience, who are all watching her.*)

I want to apologize to all of you, every one of you, for the way I made the request for help for the orphans' home on Sunday after the play. I know I was wrong to demand anything from you good people. I want your forgiveness for letting my temper out. I am sorry from the bottom of my heart. Please forgive me. I see Mr. George Simpson sitting near the back. It's up to him whether we get the house for the orphans, but I am sure the Lord will take care of the little children.

(*Mandie feels her knees about to fold up and she starts to return to her seat.*)

(*The people in the church begin murmuring.*)

(*The man who started it all suddenly walks up to the pulpit. He steps in front of Mandie to speak.*)

MAN

I must ask your forgiveness, Miss Amanda Shaw. I am terribly sorry for my stupid outburst last Sunday. You are trying to do a wonderful thing, and I was trying to stop you. I am sorry. And to show I mean it, I have the first hundred dollars right here for the work on the house. And I will do any job that I am capable of doing to help get things going.

(*He waves the money in the air.*)

(Before Mandie can reply, the audience becomes noisy and yells such things as "Here's mine," "I'll do my part," "What can I do?" etc.)

MANDIE

(Smiles at the people.)

I love you all.

(The crowd suddenly surges forward toward the platform. They begin filling the collection plates on the table with their money.)

(Suddenly the piano blasts out with the old hymn, "Count Your Blessings," and the people chime in with the words, "Count your blessings, name them one by one . . .")

(Mandie looks down toward the piano on the side.)

MANDIE

Joe Woodard!

(She smiles and waves at Joe playing the piano, and he laughs and plays louder still.)

(George Simpson rushes up to the platform with a paper in his hand. He hands it to Mandie.)

GEORGE

I've already had the legal work done. The house is now the orphans' home.

MANDIE

(*Grasps the piece of paper, stands on tiptoe to plant a kiss on his cheek.*)

(*Mandie waves the paper at Joe and then at Uncle Ned in the audience.*)

See what God has done!

(*The audience closes in around her with a loud "Amen."*)

(*The piano gets louder with "Count Your Blessings."*)

CURTAIN